Merry
and
Bright

The Novels of Jill Shalvis

Get a Clue
Out of This World
Smart and Sexy
Strong and Sexy
Superb and Sexy
Instant Attraction
Instant Gratification
Instant Temptation

Anthologies Featuring Jill

Bad Boys Southern Style
He's the One
Merry and Bright

Merry and Bright

JILL SHALVIS

KENSINGTON BOOKS
www.kensingtonbooks.com

KENSINGTON BOOKS are published by

Kensington Publishing Corp.
119 West 40th Street
New York, NY 10018

All Kensington titles, imprints, and distributed lines are available at special quantity discounts for bulk purchases for sales promotion, premiums, fund-raising, educational, or institutional use.

Special book excerpts or customized printings can also be created to fit specific needs. For details, write or phone the office of the Kensington Sales Manager: Kensington Publishing Corp., 119 West 40th Street, New York, NY 10018. Attn.: Sales Department. Phone: 1-800-221-2647.

Kensington and the K logo Reg. U.S. Pat. & TM Off.

ISBN-13: 978-1-4201-3417-9 (ebook)
ISBN-10: 1-4201-3417-5 (ebook)

ISBN-13: 978-1-4967-2532-5
ISBN-10: 1-4967-2532-8
First Kensington Trade Paperback Printing: October 2019

10 9 8 7 6 5 4 3

Printed in the United States of America

Contents

Finding Mr. Right

Chapter 1

For two months, Maggie Bell walked past him every day on her way out of the office, and every day she took in that tall, leanly muscled body, those incredibly well-fitted Levi's hanging low on his hips thanks to his tool belt, and forgot everything else just to take it all in.

Take *him* in.

As the guy in charge of earthquake retrofitting her office building, he usually carried a roll of architectural plans in one hand and a radio in his other as he dealt with his men, looking confident—not to mention smoking-hot—and every day she thought the same thing.

Yum.

She actually knew him, at least vaguely. Not that he'd remember, but twelve years ago they'd gone to high school together for one semester. Back then, she'd been a bookworm and a true science geek, and little had changed. Jacob Wahler had been the basketball star, a tough kid, though kind enough to be the only guy on his team to ever bother to smile at her. Twice she'd helped him with his chemistry homework, and then there'd been that one time he'd asked her to shut the door—when she'd walked in on him in a dark classroom with his hands down the jeans of a cheerleader.

God, she'd hated high school.

Twelve years, and she'd not ever looked back, but she was looking now. Jacob had gotten a little taller, and had filled out that long rangy body, which now appeared to be rock hard and clearly honed from the physicality of his job. And then there was everything from the neck up, which packed just as much sexual heat as the rest of him. Dark hair curling just past his collar, even darker eyes, olive skin, and a quick smile capable of melting Greenland faster than global warming.

But no matter how gorgeous, she reminded herself that guys like him weren't her fantasy, and never had been. She was a cerebral woman, and she went for cerebral men.

It was her thing.

Unfortunately her thing wasn't working so well. Somehow her Mr. Right always turned into Mr. Wrong, but she had other issues to worry about, such as her job.

She was lead chemist at Data Tech, a company run by two brothers, scientists who together employed other scientists on the cutting edge of technology. Tim and Scott West funded individual projects and innovative inventions that they deemed impressive and viable.

She planned on being both impressive *and* viable. In light of that goal, she'd been working on a skin care technology that acted as a drug delivery for cancer prevention treatments and gene repair agents. The idea wasn't new, it was actually in the preliminary experimental stages at many labs across the world, but no one had been consistently successful, not yet. She was close to it though, possibly within the next year or so—if Data Tech continued to fund her.

Tim and Scott had a lot to gain in her success, as they would claim the fame and fortune from it. Maggie didn't care about that, what she cared about was revolutionizing the delivery of drugs to the bloodstream. Every time she thought about it and the possibilities—treating skin cancer, for example, a method which could have saved her own mother—she felt so hopeful about the future, about saving lives, that she could hardly stand it.

What this meant, what it had meant for two long years, was work, work, and more work, and little-to-no social life—hence drooling after Jacob Wahler, aka Sexy Contractor Guy. Today alone she'd been in her lab since eight A.M., and as it was six P.M. now, her eyes were a little blurry. She knew she needed to call it a day and go home to the empty condo she'd bought last year.

Unbelievably, here it was again, a week before Christmas and she'd scarcely noticed the festive decorations all around her, much less even pulled out her own boxed tree and Christmas stocking for Santa. And really, what could Santa possibly bring her anyway?

A man . . .

That thought came out of nowhere but it was true. She wanted a man for Christmas. She realized it was sexist and anti-feminist, and set women back decades but she didn't care. She was a chemist, a woman with a brain who knew how to use it, and she was using it now to wish for a man.

Tonight she'd settle for a man-made orgasm . . .

Wow, she was more tired than she'd thought, and she slipped out of her lab coat, flipped off the lights in the lab, and headed into her connecting office. There she shut her laptop and slid it into her briefcase. She was going to go home, find her Christmas decorations, and get festive. Maybe sip some eggnog and try to figure out how to get un-alone. She walked out of her office and into the construction zone as she headed toward the elevators and told herself in the grand scheme of things, she was fine. Fine.

Fine.

Okay, that was a few too many fines, but she really was.

"Hey, Mags." Scott West, boss number one, poked his head out of his office, having to peer around a ladder. He was very cute, which usually made her dizzy if she looked at him too long. He wore a white lab coat over his expensive Hugo Boss shirt and pants, looking like a very expensive Doogie Howser. He was a nice catch, and they'd gone out once several weeks back, and that had been really nice, too. But then he'd gone traveling, and she'd been buried in her lab testing and reporting on the results, and . . . and they'd not gotten together again.

"Did you get a look at the showroom today?" he asked.

The showroom was on the lobby floor, filled with all the inventions Data Tech had funded, like the rainmaker that harvested water from the air, a motorized pool lounger, a human exoskeleton that could carry heavy loads over long distances, snorkel radio gear, lightbulb sheets, and any of a hundred other wild and crazy things.

"There's a new exhibit," he told her. "Floating furniture made with matching sets of repelling magnets. The couch can support up to two thousand pounds, can you believe it? How cool is that, a floating couch?"

"Very," she said, wondering who would want a floating couch.

He smiled. "I'm putting one in my office. They're carrying it up now. Want to stick around and see?"

Was he gearing up to finally ask her out again? Unlike Jacob, Scott *was* her type. She knew this. He was cerebral, brilliant really, and extremely into science, which made him perfect.

"Hey." This from boss number two, who poked his head out of *his* office, right next to his brother's.

They were identical twins. Crazily competitive twins, with Tim into robotics and Scott into molecular bionics. They ran

Data Tech as a legacy to their father, while each doing their damnedest to one up the other, at work, at play, in any way they could.

Tim tossed a glass vial to Maggie. Her latest formula, which she'd given him a few days ago. "It's beautiful," he told her. "But we've added a secret ingredient. Let us know what you think."

She held the vial up to the light but didn't see any change. "What is it?"

"Tim," Scott said, suddenly looking unhappy. "I—"

"Just something to smooth the formula," Tim said over Scott. "It's a secret until you let us know if you like it."

"I'll try it out tonight." She'd been running test groups on the drug delivery formula using Vitamin B3 and other essential oils as the drug of choice. So far, she'd been inconsistently successful, but she *would* get there.

"Tim." Scott sent his brother a long look. "I thought we— you know I wanted to . . ."

"Spit it out, bro."

But Scott appeared to have lost his words, and just glanced at his brother.

"Lethologica," Maggie said. "The state of not being able to find the word you want." She patted Scott's arm. "Don't worry, it happens to me all the time, it'll pass."

Scott blinked and she smiled, but he didn't return it. "I'll test it for you," he said instead, reaching for the vial. "No need for you to have to."

"Oh, no, that's okay. I don't mind at all."

"She doesn't mind," Tim said to Scott. "Let it go. 'Night, Maggie."

Maggie looked at Scott, who clearly wasn't going to ask her out now. " 'Night."

"Maggie." Scott eyed the vial. "I really think—"

" *'Night,*" Tim repeated, putting a hand over his twin's face and pushing him back into his office. "Don't have too much fun tonight, Maggie."

Okay, they were acting strange. But who was she to judge? As for having fun, ha. After a lifetime of being the nerd, of going to Stanford three years ahead of her peers, of completing college before anyone her age had even begun, she'd gotten damn good at *not* having fun.

And wasn't that just the problem.

Turning, she walked to the elevator. She could see Jacob and his crew at work, just down the hall. He stood on a ladder, pulling a hammer out of his tool belt, reaching far above him to a ceiling tile, that long, hard body all stretched taut . . .

The elevator dinged and she stepped into it, craning her neck, not to see all the pretty decorations, but to catch the last view of Jacob's tush as the doors slid shut. Was Scott's butt that cute? Since he always wore a white lab coat, she couldn't say.

Outside, she drew in a breath of the cool L.A. evening air and headed to her car as her cell phone rang. It was her sister Janie, a UCLA professor who did *not* have the geek gene. Nope, Janie had somehow snagged a normal life for herself. She'd married and brought two beautiful kids into the world, and was determined to make sure Maggie did the same.

"Hey, Mags." Janie's mouth was clearly full. "Sorry, chocolate stuck in my teeth."

"Don't tell me you're still eating leftover Halloween candy."

"A Baby Ruth bar. Sinful, I'm telling you. Why do you think they call it a Baby Ruth? Why not a Baby Jane or something?"

"It was supposedly named for Grover Cleveland's baby daughter."

"Your brain works in the oddest ways."

"I know."

"Uh-huh. And do you also know if you're coming for Christmas Eve?"

"Bringing the pumpkin pie."

"Spending the night?"

"Wouldn't want to miss Santa."

A lie, and they both knew it. Maggie just didn't want to be alone in her condo on Christmas morning. "What am I supposed to get you for Christmas, by the way? You already have everything you could want."

"You could bring a date."

When Maggie laughed, Janie sighed. "Well, you could *try.* Your Mr. Right is just right around the corner, I know it."

"Yes, but which corner?" Maggie stopped beside her sensible Toyota and searched for her keys, blowing out an irritated breath when she realized she was completely blocked in by Tim's *not* sensible Porsche. "Dammit." She whirled back to the building. "I have to go kill my boss."

"Invite someone from work," Janie said. "Not the boss you're going to kill, but the other one."

"I want *him* to ask *me* out. But my Mr. Rights all seem gun shy."

"Then invite a Mr. Wrong."

"You mean *purposely* go out with someone who isn't right for me?"

"Honey, you've gone two years without sex. What do you have to lose by changing tactics? I mean, honest to God, your good parts are going to wither from nonuse."

"Well, what am I supposed to do, just take off my clothes and have wild sex with the first guy I come across?"

"Yes," Janie said. "The first *wrong* guy, the one you wouldn't normally go out with."

"You want me to have sex with Mr. Wrong."

"Use a condom."

Maggie laughed. "You can't be serious."

"Seriously serious. You need to go for the first Mr. Wrong to cross your path—as long as he's not an ax murderer or rapist," she qualified. "And probably he should have a job and love his mother. *That* can be my Christmas present—you having sex with Mr. Wrong. Promise me."

Since that was as unlikely to happen as having sex with a Mr. Right, Maggie laughed as she walked back into the building. Back on the sixth floor, she dodged through the obstacle course of construction equipment. The construction crew was desperately trying to finish before Christmas, and apparently they were working late tonight. Still on the phone with her sister, she ducked under a ladder, over a cord, and then around a huge stack of unused drywall, catching her shoulder on the sharp edge. She heard the rip of her coat and sighed as she dropped her briefcase to look. *"Dammit."*

"What?" Janie asked. "Mr. Wrong?"

"No! Jeez. Hold on." She bent for her briefcase, just as someone beat her to it, scooping up the loose change that had spilled out.

"Thanks—" Maggie lifted her head and froze at the wide chest in her vision.

A chest that once upon a time she'd dreamed about in chemistry. She took the coins from Jacob's big, work-roughened palm, her nerves suddenly crackling as well as all the good spots Janie had mentioned, which meant that they hadn't withered up, at least not yet. "Three quarters, four dimes, and four pennies," she said. "$1.19."

"That's fast math."

Yes, her brain always sped up when she was anxious. Plus, there was the other thing. She was also a little revved up. Sexually speaking. Which was Janie's fault, she decided, for putting the idea of hot sex in her head in the first place. "A dollar and nineteen cents is the largest amount of money in coins you can have and still not be able to make change for a dollar."

He blinked, then nodded. "That's . . . inter—esting."

"It's fact." Oh, God. *Shut up.*

"Who's that?" Janie whispered in her ear. "Who are you talking to? A man? It's got to be a man because you're spouting off useless trivia like you do when you're nervous. Oh! He's your Mr. Wrong, isn't he? *Ask him to have hot sex with you!*"

"Hush," Maggie said, and Jacob blinked again. Oh, God. "Not you." She stood, and he did the same, giving her a quick peek of him close up and personal. His scuffed work boots, the mile-long legs and lean hips, covered in Levi's, all faded and stressed white in all the right places, of which there appeared to be a tantalizing many. God bless denim . . . "Thanks, Jacob."

At his surprise, she nodded. "Yeah, we know each other, or used to. Chem 101, your junior year at South Pasadena High. Before you moved to New Orleans."

"Maggie Bell?" His eyes warmed. "I remember now. You came up directly from eighth grade, right? You saved my ass that year."

"Jacob . . ." Janie whispered in her ear. "I don't remember a Jacob. Is he cute?"

Yeah, he was cute. Cute like a wild cheetah. As in look but don't touch. And while she stood there, still enjoying his jeans—what was with her?—her mouth ran loose. "Until you and your crew started retrofitting the building, the dress code around here was pretty much limited to white lab coats."

His mouth quirked. "I can't climb ladders in a white lab coat."

"No, no it's okay." *So okay.* "I get tired of looking at all that white anyway. So it's good that you're not." *Oh, just shut up already!* "Wearing one," she added weakly.

"You should probably not talk anymore," Janie said, ever so helpfully over the phone.

Maggie bit her lip to keep it shut. He was so close, so big. And she felt a little like a doe caught in the headlights.

"You tore your coat," he said, and fingered the hole.

At his touch, her body tightened, and her mouth opened again. "It's okay. I tend to do things like this a lot."

"Run into drywall?"

"Run into stuff, period." Someone had opened a window, and the evening breeze came in, as well as the sounds from the street six floors below. Traffic, an airplane, a sudden blare of a horn so loud she jumped.

"Just a car," he said.

"In the tone of an F."

"Excuse me?"

"All car horns are in the chord of F."

He did that eyebrow arch thing again.

"Jesus, Mags. *Stop talking!*" Janie demanded in her ear.

"Okay, I've really got to go."

"Wait!" Janie yelled. "Ask him out first, you promised! You have to do him, and get him to do you—"

Maggie slapped her phone shut before Jacob could hear her crazy sister. Yes, he was Mr. Wrong. Wrong, wrong, wrong. But what was she supposed to do, say *Hey, how do you feel about me jumping your bones?* Probably she should start with a dinner invite and work her way up to the jumping bones part. Yeah, that was it, that was how *normal* women did these things. Okay. She took both a big breath and a small step backward for distance, but Jacob curled his fingers into the front of her jacket and caught her up against him.

Not that she was complaining, but . . . "Um—"

He gestured to the bucket of nails she'd nearly stepped in, and she winced. His body, plastered to hers, was as hard as it appeared. And warm. Very, very warm. "Thanks."

"Maybe you should just stand real still," he suggested, and let go of her.

"Yes, except I don't stand still very well. I only do still when I'm lying down."

He arched a brow, those deep chocolate brown eyes lighting up with amusement to go with the heat still there, making her realize the double entendre she'd just said. "You know what I mean."

He just smiled, and turned his head toward a crew member who came up to him with a McDonald's bag.

"Burgers on the run." Jacob took the food. "Thanks."

Maggie's mouth once again ran away from her brain. "There're one hundred seventy-eight sesame seeds on each of those hamburger buns."

He leaned back against the wall, all casual like, in direct contrast to her uptightness. "One hundred seventy-eight, huh?" He was clearly biting back a smile. "Exactly?"

"Or thereabouts," she muttered, wondering how it was she could be so smart and yet not be able to keep her mouth shut.

"So you graduated early to become a sesame seed counter?"

"No." She laughed. "No. I'm sort of a chemist."

"How does one become a *sort of* chemist?"

Yeah, still amusing him. Terrific. Just what she wanted to do, amuse the gorgeous man, at her own expense. "Okay, it's not sort of. It's really. I'm really a chemist." Wow, so much better. Now all she had to do to complete her humiliation was ask him out. No sweat. "So—"

But he pushed away from the wall, calling out to one of his workers. "Dave, not there, over a foot! Check the specs!" He glanced back at Maggie. "Do me a favor and watch where you walk in here tonight."

Yes, she'd just watch where she was going, she thought with a sigh as he walked away. That was her. Always watching. Never doing. She opened Tim's office door. "Your car's in my way."

He looked up with concern. "You didn't bump it?"

"No, of course not."

He rushed off to check on his precious baby, and Maggie followed at a slower pace, calling back her sister as she went. "He walked away from me."

"Who, your Mr. Wrong? Did you ask him out?"

"No, I ran out of words."

"You tell him that car horns are in the chord of F and you can't find the words to ask him out? God, you need help."

"I know!"

Chapter 2

When the alarm went off well before dawn, Jacob groaned, squelched the urge to toss the thing out his window, and rolled out of bed. He strode naked to the shower, which he cranked up to scalding.

This eighty-hour workweek shit had to stop.

After pulling on his last set of clean clothes—damn, he really needed a night at home to catch up—he headed to work, already on his cell phone with his crew, who wanted to get this job finished as badly as he did. He wanted to fly to New Orleans as scheduled in two days, hang out with his family, and possibly do the stacked blonde his brother had set him up with for New Year's Eve.

Simple needs, really. Except there was a glitch. Christ, he hated glitches, and he had the mother of all glitches staring him in the face. He had to finish this job before anyone could leave. He'd signed a contract with Data Tech and he had two days left on that contract. Two days or he'd lose his ten percent bonus—only thanks to delay after delay, they had at least a week's worth of work still to be done in that two days.

Not good odds, but then again, he'd faced worse. Much worse.

He left his house, skirted the jammed L.A. freeways like a pro, and was on the job before the sun had even thought about coming up. And since he had a kick-ass crew, they'd joined him without complaint.

Okay, there was complaining, but they all wanted that ten percent bonus as badly as he did, so they bitched and worked at the same time. After they finished this building, they were jumping right into another job on Fourth Street. Business was good. Actually, business was great.

So why he felt so damn restless, he really had no idea. Maybe the trip would help. He could see his mom and sister, and make sure they were doing okay in their new place. He could see his brother and catch up.

And get laid.

Yeah. All systems go on that one. After moving to New Orleans in his senior year of high school, he'd come back out to Los Angeles five years ago with his best friend and partner, Sam. They'd started out in the hole, practically having to beg, borrow, and steal jobs, but they'd managed. And then they'd gotten their first big contract, and that had led to two more, and they'd been on their way.

Then Sam had gone home for his brother's birthday and had gotten killed in Katrina, and things hadn't been the same for Jacob since. He'd been left with five large contracts already signed, when all he'd wanted to do was go home and wallow. In hindsight, those jobs had probably saved his sorry ass. Even if this one just might kill him. But he wanted that damn bonus. It'd help both his mother and sister pay off the mortgages on homes that no longer even existed, and it would ease their tight financial situation.

He was busy laying out some electrical lines when he heard the *click click clicking* of heels and knew it was 8:03 exactly, because at 8:03 every single morning, she appeared. Maggie Bell, his new favorite "sort of" chemist with the encyclopedia brain filled with odd facts.

She'd grown up. Filled out. And looked damn good. She wore black pumps today, her long legs covered in sheer silk, a business skirt and blouse, and since it was December and chilly, an overcoat, open and flapping behind her as she rushed along, working her cell phone, sipping her caffeine, and balancing a briefcase. She looked a little bit harried, a little bit late, and in spite of the fact that she screamed class, also just a little bit messy.

God, he loved that part. He had a feeling if the right guy came along and took that pen out from behind her ear, then slid his fingers into her hair and kissed her long and hard and wet, she'd melt. That fantasy alone had gotten him through the past two months.

As he did every single morning, he stopped whatever he was doing to watch. She didn't disappoint. Today her honey-colored hair was piled on top of her head in what looked to be a precarious hold. She didn't wear much makeup that he could tell, but her lips were glossed. Her eyes were covered by reflective sunglasses but he knew them to be a light blue, and that in five seconds they'd focus in on him and she'd stumble just a little. Then her mouth would tremble open in a perfect little O, and time would stop, just literally stop.

And then she'd blink. Her eyes would cool, as if she'd just remembered that they were virtual strangers. She'd pretend to be occupied by something in her hands and rush into her lab, not to be seen again until at least six—

Ah, there it was. She glanced up, saw him only a few yards away with the electrical wiring in his hands. She came to an abrupt halt, prompting two of his guys behind her to nearly plow into her.

Her mouth opened and apologies tumbled out from everyone,

and then his guys made their way around her and she gripped her things, once again turning her head in his direction, this time with a hint of pink in her cheeks.

He lifted his hand and waggled his fingers.

Her mouth curved in a self-deprecatory smile. "Whoops." Her voice was soft and musical, and if he'd let it, it would have gone straight to his head. And other places.

In high school, she'd been the quietest little thing. He remembered sitting near her, watching her absorb school in a way he'd never quite managed. He'd actually wished he could be more like her. She'd helped him out, and he'd been grateful, but she'd been too shy to get to know, not to mention far too young. And then he'd moved and had never seen her again.

He was seeing her now—warm eyes, sweet smile, and a body made for sin. Not too young now, was she . . . ?

Scott West came out of the elevator, dressed like a man who didn't have to worry about any ten-percent potential profit loss. "Hey, Maggie," he said. "Jacob."

Scott had been a tough-ass at the negotiating table, but was looking much softer now that he was taking in Maggie's sweet morning appearance. "So what's today's fact?" he asked her, flashing a set of perfect teeth.

"Odontophobia," she said, staring at his extremely white teeth. "The fear of teeth. Point one percent of the population suffers from it."

Scott laughed and shook his head. "Good one. So . . . about that vial Tim gave you—"

"Oh! I tried it last night. The secret ingredient . . . it's sweet almond oil, right? For that extra vitamin E? It's a little too thick now but I'll—"

"No, no, don't worry about it. I'll have Tim rework it." He held out his hand, presumably for said vial, but she shook her head.

"It's at my condo, sorry."

"Gotcha. Well . . ." He opened his office door with a smile not quite the same wattage as before. "See you at the staff meeting."

Maggie turned back to Jacob, but stopped short when her cell phone rang. With a look of apology, she opened her bag and pulled it out to answer it. Immediately a frown crossed her brow, and she forgot about him, he could tell. She was on the move again, talking, gesturing with her full hands, not watching where she was going as she headed beneath his scaffolding to enter her lab, just barely ducking as two men from his crew moved a heavy piece of equipment in front of her.

The woman was a walking/talking accident just waiting to happen. The cutest, sexiest, walking/talking accident he'd ever seen.

Maggie spent the entire morning hunched over her laptop, going over lab results, ignoring a flood of pesky texts from a nosy-body Janie.

Alice showed up at noon with lunch. "Men suck," she said, handing a wrapped sandwich to Maggie. "And I think the bottle for your cream should be blue."

Alice was twenty-two, an intern on loan from UCLA to do Data Tech's filing, but she'd latched onto Maggie because she wanted to be a scientist, too. Dressed like a Goth superhero, all in black and lace, with some interesting deep purple lipstick, she sighed glumly as she sat and opened her sandwich. "I think my boyfriend is cheating on me with his lab partner."

"Oh, Alice. I'm sorry."

"Yeah." Alice usually wore an expression of general angry-at-the-world emo-ism. But today there was something new, hurt. "Me, too. But definitely blue glass. For your cream. My grandmother loves blue glass."

Talking with Alice made her dizzy. "I'm aiming for a younger crowd here."

"Hey, my grandmother is a tough chick. She rides with the

Hells Angels, and is armed to the teeth at all times. And isn't it a wrinkle cream?"

Maggie looked into Alice's face, which was gorgeous, smooth, and covered in pale, pale foundation. "Yes, I've made several wrinkle creams. But I'm also working on a drug delivery system. And trust me, you're only a few years away from your first wrinkle."

"I am not. I don't allow my skin to touch the sun. Haven't you heard? Goth is the new tan." She took a big bite of her PB&J. "The drug delivery system thing is cool. I should start reading the reports I'm filing for you guys."

Scott poked his head in the lab, his gaze passing over Alice to meet Maggie's. "Lunch?"

Maggie had been waiting so long to have him ask her out again it almost seemed surreal. She was crazy not to jump up and say "yes!" but the fact was, Scott was a Mr. Right and she'd given up Mr. Rights. Thanks to Janie, she was going to go for her Mr. Wrong.

Soon as she figured out exactly how to do that. She held up her half-eaten sandwich. "Sorry, I'm almost done."

He nodded, nonchalantly looking around her lab, as if not sure what to do with himself. "Well, okay then. See you later."

When he was gone, Alice looked at Maggie. "He wants into your pants."

"Because he offered me lunch?"

"Yeah, I think you should go for it. He's rich and he's hot. And *rich*. Which always trumps hot. My boyfriend's rich. Or his family is." Some of her perpetual anger made room for that hurt again. "Unfortunately he's also a dick."

Maggie squeezed her hand in sympathy. "Neither hot nor rich are important criteria for me."

Alice seemed baffled by this. "What's more important than rich?"

Maggie sighed. "Scott's my type."

"The bastard."

"No, I mean . . . I'm trying a new thing. I'm going for the *opposite* of my type. I'm going for Mr. Wrong."

Alice put down her sandwich. "Okay, this is interesting. Go on."

"It's my sister's idea. She made me promise that my Christmas present to her would be me ignoring all the Mr. Rights and going for Mr. Wrong."

"So have you found him yet?"

Maggie hesitated, and Alice pounced with glee. "You have, haven't you?" She grinned. "Who is he, that geek in accounting—what's his name, the one who actually carries pencils and pens and a calculator in his shirt pocket?"

"Alan, and he's a great guy, but no. He's not a Mr. Wrong, he's . . ." Her own type. The overeducated thinker, nice but distracted, and to be honest, a little aloof. She wanted passion, she wanted aggression, she wanted . . . *wild sex.*

Oh, God, it was true. She wanted wild sex from her Mr. Wrong. "I'm not really ready to share."

Alice sighed and packed up the trash from lunch. "Fine. It's none of my business and it's going to end badly anyway, these things always do."

"Alice—"

"I have to go. It's time to get filing. Hey, maybe I'll learn something."

Maggie got back to work. At the end of the day, she closed up and left her lab. The place was completely void of Data Tech employees, which was typical of Christmas week. Everyone wanted to rush home to their families.

Their significant others.

She sighed again and kept walking, trying not to notice the boughs of holly, the lights . . . the noise of the construction workers. Two of them were mumbling about the long night ahead and their looming deadline, and she wondered if their boss was still in the building. Maybe like *her* boss, Jacob had deserted his workers. Maybe he was home drinking eggnog with his friends, enjoying the holiday; maybe he was on a date, which for some reason tightened a knot in her gut and made her head hurt. She rubbed her forehead and—

And tripped over an open toolbox, hitting the floor on all fours. Her briefcase went flying, and the pen she'd forgotten she had behind her ear skittered across the floor. "Dammit."

"So much for watching where you're going."

Accompanying this most annoying statement, two big, warm hands gripped her waist and hoisted her up. When she tilted her head back, her gaze collided with a set of dark brown eyes. Terrific. *Now* he showed up. She bent to look at her burning knees, which were both skinned good and already starting to bleed. *"Dammit."*

"You said that." Jacob crouched down, seeming big and bad and just a little irritated. He had drywall dust and sawdust all over him, and was hot and sweaty, and clearly not exactly thrilled at the interruption. He picked up all her things, easily tucking them beneath one arm. "Shit, you're bleeding," he said, looking at the trickle running down her calf. "Tommy, bring me a clean rag!"

"It's okay." She sucked in a painful breath. Liar, liar . . .

But she smiled into his solemn eyes as her heart kicked hard. "The human heart can create enough pressure to squirt blood thirty feet, so this is nothing, relatively speaking." Even if her knees were on fire . . . "I'm fine," she said, and stood up.

He straightened, too, and she suddenly became aware of exactly how close they were. Inches apart, which was waaaay closer than they'd ever been. Someone, presumably Tommy, tossed him a rag, which he caught over her head and handed to her.

"Thanks." She hadn't skinned her knees in years and she didn't remember it hurting this bad. She dabbed at her knees and hissed out a breath. "You don't by any chance have a Band-Aid? Or two?"

"Sure do." He led her down the hall, past the elevators. The building was in a U-shape, curved around a courtyard six stories below. Out of the corner of her eye, she watched him walk, his broad shoulders stretching the seams of his shirt, his Levi's lovingly cupping a most drool-worthy butt.

Odd to be so attracted to a Mr. Wrong, but her body was humming again in spite of her knees. He hadn't gotten himself a haircut, and the dark strands of his hair looked soft and silky. He hadn't shaved that morning, and maybe not yesterday morning either, and that growth didn't look soft and silky at all. It would be rough against her skin, which for some reason, gave her a little shiver. "I was wondering . . ." *If I could ask you to do me.*

Still walking, he glanced over at her. His jaw was square, his mouth generous, but it was his eyes that held her. They were fathomless, and in those swirling depths was a mix of emotions with a barely restrained impatience leading the pack. He was busy, needing to get back to work, and at the knowledge, her nerve packed up and went on vacation. "Never mind."

Two years without sex, her good parts whined. . . .

They turned a corner, tight with stacks of boxes. "Watch where you're going," Jacob reminded her.

Right. Watch where she was going instead of watching him and daydreaming. Time to stop daydreaming! "Yes, well, in my defense, I rarely do watch where I'm going."

"And we've got a mess all around you, I know. But your boss promised he'd give you all this week off so we'd have the empty building to ourselves. Then he didn't."

"Tim's a good guy, but he's tight with his money, so tight he squeaks when he walks." She smiled when he laughed. He had a good laugh. "He's never given us a week off."

"We're attempting to not miss our deadline. Some of us have flights to catch out of here tomorrow, if we finish."

"You'll finish."

He looked a little surprised, and a little amused. "How do you know?"

She was doing her best not to limp. No limping in front of the cute guy from high school—but she wanted to. "In high school, you finished everything you started, even when it was hard. Basketball, chemistry . . ." *The 36-D blonde in that empty classroom . . .* God, she'd been so jealous of that girl. "You just seem like a guy who still finishes what he starts."

His eyes heated, and oh, Lord, so did her body, but had she really just said he looked like a guy who finished what he started? Why didn't she just strip down right here and ask him to finish her? "Where are you flying out to?" she asked instead, desperate for a subject change. "New Orleans?"

"You remember."

She remembered everything about him, but gave a slight shrug. Playing it cool.

"My mom lost her house in Katrina," he said. "She's in a new place now and we're all meeting there for Christmas."

"Sounds lovely." She was happy for him, but wistful for herself. Yes, she had Janie, but she missed having her mom, too.

Jacob stopped at an empty lab on the far side of the building, which he and his crew used as an office and for tool storage. Knees on fire, Maggie sat on a chair while he dug into a large toolbox and came up with a first-aid kit.

"Here's some antiseptic spray," he said. "It'll take out the sting. Pull up your skirt."

No can do. Not when she'd just remembered she hadn't shaved her legs. "I'll do it." She held out her hand for the spray, which she shoved beneath her skirt, gave a cursory spritz and gritted her teeth. "All better."

"Maggie, I can see the blood dripping down your calves. This is my fault, so let me see."

"I'm good."

With a sigh, he reached for the hem of her skirt himself.

Chapter 3

Jacob's fingers brushed Maggie's skirt, and suddenly he wasn't thinking about her knees but other things altogether, until Maggie put her hands over his, flashing a quick and definitely fake smile. "I just remembered. I have my own Band-Aids."

He pushed a smile of his own, one that usually got him a lot more than a peek at an injured knee. "Maggie, it's just your knees."

"It's not my knees I'm worried about."

She was blushing. Was she for real? He had a million other things to do, and yet he was crouched before her watching her most mesmerizing face. She was the ultimate science geek fantasy, if one was into that sort of thing. And apparently, given his pheromone level whenever she got within sight, he was. Her hair was still piled on top of her head, her lips fully glossed, and that smoking body covered up with her coat. Her killer eyes were magnified behind her lab glasses, which she'd clearly forgotten to take off. She'd put the pen behind her ear again.

She flashed another fake smile and rose, then winced and sat back down. "Honestly, it's not hurting at all."

"God, you are such a liar." He shuffled through the kit. "Damn, I don't have Band-Aids. I can't believe it. Joe must have used them all last week when he staple-gunned his finger to the ceiling. The spray should help, though. Did you get a lot of it? Come on, let me see."

"Can't."

"Why not? You have ugly knees?"

She rolled her eyes. "If you must know, I didn't shave my legs."

"Jesus, really? I'll call the fashion police, stat."

She wasn't amused at his grin. "It's not funny. I haven't been as diligent lately since I'm not dating."

He sat back on his heels, fascinated by this, by her. "So you only shave your legs for a date?"

"Well, it's a time sink otherwise, and—Never mind." She lifted her chin. "My point is, I can't show you my legs if I haven't shaved them."

"Maggie, I don't care."

With a look that said she was prepared for his disgust, she finally pulled her skirt up past her knees.

His smile caught in his throat. Disgust was the last thing he felt. She was definitely wearing silk, which had torn and snagged at both knees, but that wasn't what caught his interest and held it. Nope, that honor went to the fact that her silk stopped at mid-thigh, or one did; the other had sagged down just above her bloody knee, held there by what appeared to be an inch-wide strip of stretchy lace.

If she'd been this sexy in high school, he'd been blind. He tried to control himself, but suddenly all he could think about was what she'd look like in that silk and her white lab coat and nothing else.

As if she could see his wicked, dirty little thoughts, she let out a sound that managed to convey what she thought of him, and snatched the antiseptic herself. "I got this."

"Okay." He straightened and jammed his hands in his pockets, waiting for her to deal with it, letting out a slow, long breath, practicing some multiplication problems in his head . . . anything to make sure his brain didn't focus in on those sexy as hell thigh-highs. But she slowly rolled the stocking down, past the scraped knee, and—

"Don't look!"

"I'm not."

"You are so."

Yeah, he was.

"What, you've never seen a clumsy woman tear her stockings before?"

"I've never seen a beautiful woman so unaware of herself before."

Her gaze snapped up to his, and he let her look her fill, which she did with a wary hunger that quite frankly turned him on more than the stockings, more than any woman had in a long time.

"So I have a little thing for lingerie," she said defensively, and sprayed her knees again. "And dammit, *ouch.*"

He put a hand on her thigh, bent, and blew on the scrapes.

She gasped.

Nope, he wasn't alone in this odd and inexplicable attraction. "Maggie?"

"Yeah?"

"You're crazy if you think I have a problem with your lingerie."

"It's not that I'm crazy. Although in general, women are thirty-seven percent more likely to need a psychiatrist."

That made him smile. "You know some interesting things."

"I know, it's odd. I'm . . . odd. I dress in lab coats every day and I wear glasses, and my hair—Well, just never mind about my hair. I know what I look like. Wearing sexy underwear gives me the illusion of *being* sexy, at least in my own mind."

He took in her slightly disheveled, sexy-as-hell appearance and shook his head. "Hate to argue with someone thirty-seven percent more likely to need professional help, but there's no illusion here. You *are* sexy as hell."

She blushed beet red. "And not that it's any of your business, but the thigh-highs are far better for the female body anyway, and—" She broke off when he slipped his hand around the back of one calf and lifted her leg enough to get a good look at her trashed knees.

"And . . . ?" he prompted, when she didn't finish.

"And . . ." She slid her eyes to his hand on her. "I lost my train of thought."

"You were talking about your lingerie fetish."

She pushed him back a step. "It's not a fetish!"

"Okay."

"It's not!" She shook her head and let out a breath. "Oh, forget it." She thrust the antiseptic spray at him and got up. As she straightened her legs, she sucked in another breath.

"Still hurt?"

"It's just scraped knees." She shoved her nose up into nosebleed heights. "I'll be fine." She put a hand to his chest to push him out of her way, then frowned down at her hand.

"Yeah," he said, feeling the pull at the touch. "Quite a punch, huh?"

"What's quite a punch?"

"The chemistry. Our chemistry. Fitting, I think, since chemistry is where we first met."

She paused. "You think we have chemistry?"

"I guess it could be static electricity."

She choked out a laugh, looking down at her fingers, still spread over his chest. "Do you remember me catching you in that empty classroom with that girl?"

He went blank a moment, then grimaced. "Oh, shit. Yeah. Look, in my defense, I was an idiot back then."

She limped to the window, which looked over the courtyard, and farther, back to her own lab. "Hey, my light's on," she said with surprise. "I didn't leave my light on."

"Maybe you forgot."

"No. I shut down my laptop, locked my files, filled my briefcase with everything I need to work at home tonight, and then shut off my light. Like I do every single night."

"It happens."

"Not to me." She took a hobbling step toward the door, and he sighed. "Give me your keys. I'll run back and flip it off for you."

She hugged her keys to her chest. "That would be against the rules."

"And you always follow the rules. Even if your gut tells you otherwise."

"Well, yes."

"Doing my homework for me was against the rules."

"I didn't look at it like that." She sagged a little. "I was trying to help you, and . . ."

"And?"

"And I had a crush on you. Which you had to know."

He paused, then let out a breath. "Yeah, but like I said, I was an idiot back then."

"No, I think you're onto something. Not about breaking the rules, but about following your gut. I need to do that for this situation." She looked very determined. "Follow my gut."

"Which situation?"

She hesitated.

"Tell me."

"You're very different," she said. "Direct."

"Saves a lot of time. Save time, Maggie."

"Okay, if you must know, I'm determined to need to shave my legs more often. How's that for direct? But not for my usual Mr. Right, because my usual Mr. Right always turns out to be Mr. Wrong. Using reverse psychology, when I shave my legs, it's going to be for a Mr. Wrong, and a night I won't easily forget. One night, and then we both just walk away. Do you understand?"

He blinked. "You need a razor."

With a frustrated sound, she walked out of the lab. He followed her limping form back down the hallway. "At least let me give you a lift."

"No, I'm good."

He watched her hobble another moment, then grabbed her, and turning his back to her, bent at the knees and hoisted her up.

"Hey—"

"Just a piggyback, relax." Which he realized was going to be next to impossible for the woman who probably never relaxed, just as she never broke the rules.

"Don't touch my legs."

How did a woman like this even have sex? "Hold on," he commanded, locking her hands together across his chest.

"Oh, God."

Yeah. If their *accidental* touch had set off sparks, there was a fire blazing now that she had her breasts smashed to his back and her legs around his waist. He lowered his hands to her thighs to hold her up. Her skirt was long and gauzy, and stretchy enough that she wasn't flashing anyone behind him. Her modesty was perfectly intact, except for the fact that her crotch was pressed against his lower back, but he decided not to mention that.

But he felt it, felt the heat of her, and suddenly he needed to do some relaxing of his own, especially when he spread his fingers to touch as much of her as he could and she shivered, pressing her forehead to his shoulder.

He understood. But it was one thing to fantasize about the pretty scientist geek, and another entirely to think about doing more than just fantasizing.

As he strode with her down the hallway, a few of his men gave him a second look, some even taking a third and fourth look. No one said a word, though, as he carried her, trying not to enjoy the feel of her legs hugging his hips, her breasts up against his back, and utterly failing as he took her past the offending toolbox and to her closed lab.

Which was locked up tighter than a drum.

"Key's in my pocket," she said in his ear.

He slid a hand to her hip, and she sucked in a breath. "I'll get it!"

"Okay, okay. Just trying to help you out."

"Letting me down would be helping me out."

"Sure." He loosened his hold on her legs, allowing her to slide down his back, making sure it was a slooowwwww slide, because there was something about having her legs wrapped around him, about the heat between those legs—

"You have a dirty mind," she said.

"Hey, I didn't say a word."

"You were thinking it. You were thinking about us . . ."

"Yes?"

"Having sex," she whispered.

"We'd both have to be facing the other way for that."

"Argh," she responded, or something close to that, and dug into her own pockets for her key. She unlocked the door, flipped on the lights, and nearly shut the door in his face when he didn't step inside fast enough. "I've got it from here, thanks."

"Just wanted to see your world." He stepped into the room, which was as neat and tidy as he imagined it would be. There was a long table against one wall, lined with microscopes and other various equipment, another worktable along a second wall, with sinks and burners and lights, and a center workstation, behind which sat a neat black chair and a white lab coat over the back of it.

"Home sweet home," she said, and strode toward the center workstation. "Thanks for the TLC, good night."

"What's your hurry, you have your Mr. Wrong waiting for you at home?"

The tips of her ears went pink. "I shouldn't have told you. In any case, I changed my mind."

"Look at that, you're lying again."

"I . . ." She flipped on another light. "Okay, yes, I'm lying."

"Why? Am I your Mr. Wrong?"

"What?" She whipped back to face him, dropping her keys.

One look at her face had him letting out a surprised laugh. "Me? Really?"

"You were only guessing." She let out a breath and shook her head at herself. "Of course you were only guessing."

Fascinated, he moved in close. "So what exactly was it that you wanted from your Mr. Wrong?"

"Nothing. Because trust me, I'm so over it." And with that, she walked out of the lab, into a connecting bathroom, whose door she shut and locked.

Chapter 4

Maggie stared at herself in the small mirror over the bathroom vanity. "You are an idiot." She opened a drawer, searched around, and *yes,* found her own damn Band-Aids. Then she pulled out her cell and called Janie. "You're *not* getting a Christmas present."

"Oh, no. You promised. You're going to do Mr. Wrong."

"I am not going to have hot sex with that man. He's . . ." *Gorgeous. Hot.* "Insufferable."

Jacob's voice came through the door. "I'm not insufferable during hot sex, I promise."

Dammit! "I've got to go," she hissed to Janie. Red as a beet, she opened the door and found Jacob sitting on one of the worktables, a big mixing bowl on one side, toying with her electric mixer on his other. He held up a thistle tube and dropper. "I feel like we're back in chem lab."

She just looked at him, tall, big, and rough-and-tumble, a bull in her china shop. She couldn't help but picture them back in chem lab, where she'd once dreamed of him clearing the workstation with one swooping hand, then laying her down and—

He hopped off the table and patted the spot he'd just vacated. "Come here."

When she didn't, he merely scooped her up himself and put her on the counter himself.

"Hey—"

Taking the Band-Aids from her fingers, he tore one open and smiled at her as he took ahold of the hem of her skirt. "It's like we're playing doctor."

She slapped at his hand, which didn't deter him. "We are *not* playing doctor."

"Spoilsport." He pushed her skirt up above her knees and put on the Band-Aids, during which time she became hyperaware of the feel of his fingers on her skin, of the fact that when he was bent over her that way, she could smell his soap and absorb the heat of his body. But mostly she became aware of her own breathing and how it'd quickened, but once he'd finished and yet left his hands on her, the opposite happened and she stopped breathing entirely. "You listened to my conversation with my sister."

"Yes."

"This is a little awkward."

"Not for me."

Dammit. "Okay, so you were my Mr. Wrong of choice."

"Because . . ."

She grimaced, hating to admit this. "Because historically speaking, I tend to go for a certain type of guy."

"Uh-huh. Someone like yourself probably. A little anal, a little uptight—"

"Yes," she agreed, trying not to be insulted. How was it that he could be both so gorgeous and so irritating? "But it's no longer working for me. Hence the juvenile behavior of my sister and I, and me going for my Mr. Wrong in the first place. I just wanted to . . . feel. I wanted . . ."

"Hot sex."

He was smiling again, and she gritted her teeth. "Nothing permanent."

"How long has it been for you?"

"That's not really any of your business."

"How long?"

"Not quite two years." One year, eleven months, two weeks and three days, not that she was counting or anything.

"So you wanted me to be your Mr. Wrong," he said. "To break your not-quite-two-year dry spell with some hot sex." He arched his brow. "Were there any particulars? Special requests? Kinks?"

She sighed. "Do you have to be crude?"

"Oh, baby, if you think that's crude, then we're going to be in trouble when we get down to the doing."

"I'm not doing! Not with you!" She covered her face. "I'm over it."

He put a hand on either side of her hips. "But you wanted to. With me."

"Could you shut up now?" she begged. "Please?"

"I've got a better idea." His mouth nuzzled at her jaw and she attempted not to melt. "How about I keep my mouth busy with other things? God, something smells delicious."

"It's not me, it's the stuff in that mixing bowl."

He lifted the bowl. "What is it?"

"Organic honey cream. Sort of." It was a skin repair formula, and also a cell rejuvenation. Magic lotion, really.

"Organic?" There was a light in his eyes that made her nipples tingle. "As in edible?"

"I s-suppose."

"I like honey." He smiled, and it was so wicked she quivered. He dipped a finger into the bowl.

"Jacob—"

"I leave for New Orleans tomorrow, so that is your last chance at the whole Mr. Wrong experiment."

"Oh. Well. I don't think—"

Which was the last thing she got out before his mouth claimed hers. And while he distracted her with his very talented tongue, he gently urged her legs open and stepped between them, putting their bodies up flush together.

Oh, God. "This is such a bad idea," she managed as he took his lips on a tour over her jaw.

"This kind of bad is good." He took his finger, the one he'd dipped in the lotion, and touched it to her throat, then leaned in and licked it off. "Yum."

Dizzy, she clutched at him, holding him so tight to her that he couldn't have gotten away if he'd wanted to. "I really think we should take a moment and discuss this."

"Okay," he said agreeably, against her flesh. "You go ahead and discuss."

"You sh-should know, I might just be using you for the fantasy I've had since high school. The one where *I* was the girl in the empty classroom with you."

"Use me," he murmured, his tongue taking a hot lick at the dip in the hollow of her throat. "You locked the door, right?"

"No."

"I got it." He slipped the lock and kissed her again.

God, he was a great kisser. The king of great kissers. Greedy yet generous, soft yet firm, hot and wet but not too wet, and while he was going about rendering her incapable of remembering her own name, he undid the buttons on her blouse, letting out a low, appreciative throaty groan at the sight of her white lace demi bra, which was doing its job of holding up and displaying—until he unhooked it, that is. Dipping his head, he pressed his mouth to the full curves plumping out of the top of the lace as he dipped his fingers into the lotion again.

"Jacob—" The word choked off as he painted the honey lotion over her bared breasts, following up with his mouth as his very busy hands skimmed down her legs and then back up again, taking the material of her skirt up with them.

Her pulse skittered. "I don't know about—"

"You taste better than the honey."

"Thanks, but—"

"You never answered my question. Just hot sex? Or . . ." With a naughty bad boy grin, he flipped on the vibrating mixer at her hip and wriggled his eyebrows. "Extra stuff?"

She took a big gulp as he nudged her blouse off one shoulder. The soft material of his shirt was stretched taut over his leanly muscled chest, loose over his belly, which she could feel beneath her fingers, fingers that somehow slipped beneath the tee to touch warm, hard abs.

"Tell me," he said.

She played with the waistband of his jeans. "Um . . ."

"Oh, don't lose your nerve now." His mouth was at her ear. "Tell me, Maggie. Slow and sweet?" He skimmed his thumb over a nipple, making her arch into him. "Or fast and hard?" His other hand was up her skirt, playing with the edging of her panties. "Or somewhere in between?"

"Fast and hard," she decided as she shoved up his shirt, revealing his stomach, which made her mouth water. "Really fast," she choked out, as his finger slipped just beneath her panties.

"I can do fast." He glided the pad of his finger over her, his own breathing uneven, his body tight against hers.

She was breathing just as erratically, and her body was every bit as tight, and also trembling.

And wet.

She dropped her forehead to his chest. She could tell he was holding back, being careful with her, and she'd have expected that from Mr. Right but not Mr. Wrong.

She didn't want careful.

She wanted wild, unmitigated, unadulterated passion, from him, for her, and she wanted that now, along with her fast. So she kissed him, gliding her tongue to his. He made a low, rough, intimately thrilling sound from deep in his throat and his arms came up, banding tightly around her, pulling her flush to him.

Careful restraint gone. Mission accomplished.

"Tell me it's like getting back on a bike," she gasped. "That I'm going to remember what to do next."

"Trust me, you're going to remember."

"Okay." Desire was getting the best of her, and her fingers outlined the bulge of him straining the front of his jeans.

"See?" He breathed shakily. "You're remembering already."

She could hear the loud beat of his heart in her ear, could feel him shudder in pleasure when she stroked him. He wanted her. Her Mr. Wrong wanted her. Unlike her last encounter, the man she was with wasn't worrying about the time, or his next meeting, or how he looked. He was thinking of her, touching her, kissing her, completely lost in her, and she let herself get a little lost in that, lost in the heat, the passion, the need, all the things she'd deprived herself of for so long.

He tugged off her blouse, let out an extremely satisfying growl at the sight of her, and lapped up some of the honey concoction he'd left on her breasts, his thumbs rasping over her nipples until she thunked her head back against the wall. "Definitely remembering."

"Good." He laved one nipple with special, tender care, then gave the other the same attention, until her hips were rocking restlessly, needing, desperately needing. His hands danced up the back of her thighs, cupped her bottom and squeezed. "That's real good."

She tried to tug off his T-shirt, murmuring in delight when

he helped, pulling it over his head. When she leaned in to kiss his chest, he let his head fall back, his hand coming up to cup the back of hers, which tightened on her as she licked his nipple. Egged on by his shaky exhale and the way he moved hungrily against her, she did it again, lapping up his magnificent body, all lean, long, hard angles, so male, so hot. It was incredible, it was freeing, knowing this was just sex, that's all, and for that moment she felt like a different woman, and she loved it. Loved how he made her feel. "I'm ready for the fast and hard portion of the program," she whispered against his skin.

"Me, too." He urged her hand lower to prove it, helping her unzip his pants to free the essentials.

"Oh," she breathed, wrapping her fingers around him. "You've definitely got the hard part covered."

"Yeah. Let's work on the fast." Pressing his mouth to her shoulder, he hooked his fingers in her panties. "Lift up, Maggie." He tugged the material off and over his shoulder. The table was cold against her butt, making her gasp, but he slid his hands beneath her.

She'd meant to do this quick, meant to get only what she needed and get out, but suddenly, getting out was the furthest thing from her mind. Awash in sensory overload, she wanted to do this for the next hour.

All night.

Straining against him, breathing like a lunatic, she murmured in surprise when he suddenly dropped to his knees and yanked her forward.

Right against his mouth.

He kissed her then, using his tongue, his teeth, and she lost herself.

Completely.

Lost.

Herself.

When she'd stopped shuddering, he surged back to his feet, produced a condom—God bless the condom—then in the next breath filled her so full she nearly came again on impact.

And then he began to move, and she did come.

Instantaneous orgasm.

It boggled her mind, coming like that, coming without even trying, certainly without straining for it. He brought her up again with fierce thrusts that took her so far beyond her own experiences, she wasn't sure she could even bear it. But then he whispered her name in a voice that assured her she wasn't alone in this, that he was just as lost in her as she was in him.

Right there in the very lab where she'd had endless fantasies about him for the past two months, he made them all come to life. And suddenly she wasn't lost at all, but found, one-hundred-percent found.

Jacob was still trying to find his legs and gather his senses when he heard it, a soft click, like a door closing. With Maggie plopped against him like a rag doll, he lifted his head but the lab door was closed.

In his arms, Maggie stirred, and frowned. "Was that the door?"

"I thought so but—"

"No." She peeked over his shoulder. "Couldn't be. It's locked. Oh my God, do you think someone saw us?"

"Who has the key?"

She blanched and straightened. "My bosses. And probably others. But they're all gone for the day, or so I thought." She pushed at him and he released his hold on her, stepping back as she hopped down and tried to put her bra back on. "Someone was in here."

Yeah. Very likely, which pissed him off.

"But why? No one could have known we were going to . . ."

"What do you keep in here? Anything you don't want anyone to see?"

She struggled with her blouse a moment, then whirled around, snatching her panties off a microscope with a sound of distress. "Plenty."

Her answer had him taking a second look at her as she fumbled to right her skirt, which was all twisted around her waist, a hot look he might add. He knew Data Tech specialized in the latest technology and inventions, putting new and innovative things on the market, often years ahead of their competition, but he had no idea what Maggie did exactly except make edible honey lotion. She limped away and into her office, still trying to fix her clothes. "I don't know what anyone could have been looking for . . ." Then she turned back to him. "My briefcase. I left it and my purse in your temporary office—"

"Wait here." He ran back to the other side of the building, grabbed her briefcase and purse and turned to head back to her, but she'd come up behind him, standing there pale and quiet as he handed everything over.

"There's no one on my floor," she said. "No one who might have come into my lab. Everyone's office is dark." She opened up her briefcase, searching inside for . . .

A glass vial.

Looking extremely thankful to see it, she flipped through the rest of the briefcase, checked her laptop, and then took a deep sigh of intense relief.

"Important stuff?"

"Two years' worth of work, and this sample is definitely valuable enough to steal. If you know what you're looking for."

"What is it?"

"Transdermal drug delivery."

"Trans what?"

"It's a way to get cancer prevention and gene repair medication through skin care."

"Impressive," he said, staring at her, suddenly understanding exactly what someone was doing snooping in her lab. "And definitely worth stealing."

"Yes. When the formula is right, just a little bit of this stuff could deliver a critical dose of meds, and if done correctly, virtually eliminate the side effects common with injections. I'm in testing now, the dosing is still inconsistent."

"But you're close," he guessed.

"Yes. I believe I'm nearly there."

"That's amazing."

"Not yet it's not. At the moment what I've got is some fairly fabulous face cream that works better than cosmetic surgery, suitable for acne, anti-aging, and psoriasis, as well as repairing sun-damaged skin. But I'll get there."

"Is that why your skin is so amazing?"

Her gaze flew to his, startled. "You think my skin is amazing?"

He slipped his fingers into her hair, letting his thumb trace her jaw. He'd just had her, and yet the simple touch still electrified him to the core. "I do."

"It's my lotions, not me." She clasped her hands and avoided his gaze. "So . . . thanks for tonight." She grimaced. "I mean, for taking care of me after I fell, not for . . ." Her eyes drifted shut. "You know."

"For being your Mr. Wrong?"

"Well, yes." She was still flushed, her shirt a little crooked. She covered her eyes and laughed, and the sound did something low in his belly. "Look," she said. "I know this is silly but I really do want to thank you. Can I buy you a coffee?"

"Do I have to wait for you to shave your legs?"

"Ha. No, it's a little late now."

"I'd love a coffee, *and* the thanks, but I've got to get back to work. We're working through the night and all of tomorrow so we can be done in time for the holidays."

"Oh. Right." She backed up a step. "No problem." She grabbed her briefcase and purse. "I understand."

She didn't, he could tell. She thought he was rejecting her. "Maggie—"

"No, I don't want to keep you. Don't work too hard!"

And with that, she quickly rushed toward the elevator, out of sight, but not, most definitely not, out of mind.

Chapter 5

That night, Maggie was home making chocolate chip cookies and eating most of the dough before she could bake it, still unable to believe she'd had sex in her lab—her lab!—when her phone rang.

It was Scott. "Maggie?" he said, sounding caught off guard. "You're . . . home?"

"Well, yes. I am. Is there something wrong?"

"No, but . . ." He let out a laugh. "You know what? This is embarrassing. I hit the wrong number, sorry."

Click.

Maggie looked at the phone. "Okay." Good to know she wasn't the only one smart enough to calculate the mass of any object in her head but not socially talented enough to hold a conversation with the opposite sex.

And yet she'd held the attention of a man earlier, hadn't she? And even though the good-bye had been painfully awkward, everything between the Band-Aids and that awkward good-bye had been . . . perfect. She'd been wearing a stupid grin for hours. And still was. God, orgasms were good.

She should bring him some of these cookies, as that thank-you she owed him. It was the right thing to do, the polite thing to do. Thank-you-for-the-perfect-sex cookies.

Still grinning, she put a batch in the oven and ate some more dough, which made her happy, and received two prank calls, which annoyed her. She watched Letterman, which didn't annoy her, and finally went to bed, still grinning a little bit.

When she got to work the next morning, she'd managed to downgrade the grin to a smile, but as she entered the building, nerves replaced it. How was she going to look Jacob in the eye after getting naked with him? *On her worktable.* She still had the imprint of a slide on her ass. . . .

But it turned out she'd worried for nothing. While the construction equipment was still blocking most of the hallway, Jacob was nowhere in sight. If he'd worked all night long, he was probably catching a quick nap, or maybe breakfast, so she brought the container of cookies she'd made him into her office, where they proceeded to call her name all morning. By lunch she'd peeked out her door so often for a sight of her Mr. Wrong that two of his workers thought she was stalking them. Annoyed at herself, she ate a few of the cookies.

Just a few.

All afternoon she could hear Jacob's voice on the Nextels of his workers as they communicated, and every time she did, she felt the urge to eat a few more cookies.

By quitting time she'd consumed a total of seven, leaving only five.

Alice stuck her head in Maggie's door to wave good-bye and Maggie absentmindedly waved back, sneaking out one more cookie. She was thinking about the last four when Alice called her cell phone.

"Didn't you just leave?" Maggie asked her.

"I did. I am. Your car has a flat."

Dammit. She needed new tires. "Okay, I'll call Triple A, thanks."

"Call now so you don't have to wait."

"I will." She hung up and looked at the cookies. Stress. Stress made her hungry. Jacob didn't need four cookies, they were huge. So she took one more while she went back to her computer, and when she looked up again another hour had passed and the construction workers were gone.

And so was their stuff.

They were done, they were gone, and Mr. Wrong hadn't even come to say good-bye. That hurt. But it also meant that the cookies were hers, so she ate one more and called Janie. "I made Jacob a dozen cookies and ate all but two by myself. Not counting the dozen I ate last night."

"This is why you're single."

"Thanks." She hung up and took her loser self to the parking lot where she found her flat tire and remembered that she'd forgotten to call Triple A. With a sigh, she sank to the curb by her car and pulled out the Tupperware.

Yep, two cookies left.

A double loser.

Jacob had his final check in hand, including the bonus that they'd earned by the skin of their teeth. It'd been a helluva tough forty-eight hours but he was done.

Free.

Leaving Scott's office, he went by Maggie's to say good-bye before heading to the airport. He hadn't had a moment to breathe all day, but he'd thought about her. Thought about her and how she'd looked sitting on her worktable with no panties . . .

Her office was dark. He'd missed her. Frustrated, exhausted, and now disappointed, he left the building. It was a typical L.A.

winter evening, fifty-five degrees with a rare addition—clouds gathering, blocking out any moon or starlight—not that there was ever much of that visible in downtown Los Angeles anyway.

The streets were decorated with red garland and festive colored lights, along with a long string of red brake lights—business traffic trying to get to the freeway. He walked through the parking lot and came to a surprised stop in front of Maggie, sitting on the curb by her car, eating . . . a cookie? "Hey."

"Hey, yourself."

"What are you doing?"

"Eating a cookie."

"Okay." He waited for her to expand on that but she didn't.

"You can just ignore me," she said instead.

Uh-huh. As if he could. Nothing about her was ignorable, not from the tips of her toes poking out her high-heeled sandals all the way up those sweet, lush curves to the strands of her adorably messy hair. "Why are you sitting on the curb?"

"I was talking on my cell to my sister. Just doing my part of the statistic that says the average American spends two years on the phone."

"I'm not anywhere close to average."

"I know. You're bigger." She covered her face. "Sorry. Sugar rush. Too many cookies. Waaay too many."

She had a dab of chocolate on the corner of her mouth, and he found himself fixated on that. "What, no facts on cookies?"

"Oh, I have cookie facts. I was just trying to hold back."

"You don't have to hold back with me, Maggie."

"Okay. Did you know it was Ruth Graves Wakefield who first used candy-bar chocolate in a cookie recipe while at the Toll House Inn circa 1930?" She waved a cookie. "And *voilà,* chocolate chip cookies were born."

"Good one. So why are you sitting out here eating cookies?"

"Actually, technically, they're *your* cookies."

She was wearing another skirt today, a pencil skirt, with her legs demurely tucked beneath her, but he could see her knees, and the Band-Aids there. Her jacket was open over a blouse the same light blue as her eyes. She looked extremely buttoned up and extremely put together—if one didn't count her hair, which was once again defying gravity with what appeared to be a stir stick shoved into it.

And the chocolate at the corner of her mouth, let's not forget that, because he couldn't tear his eyes off of it, or understand the sudden insane urge to lean down and lick it off.

But he had his bag packed and in his truck, and a plane to catch.

Maggie took the last bite of the cookie and brushed her fingers off. "I should have baked three dozen."

"You bake?"

"Yes, and I'm good, too."

"I bet you are." He sat at her side, so tired he had no idea if he could get back up again. She smelled like chocolate. He had a feeling she would taste even better. Reaching out with his finger, he ran it over the corner of her mouth.

She pulled back. "What are you doing?"

"You have a little chocolate—"

"Oh, God." Her tongue darted out, collided with the pad of his finger. It was like an electric bolt straight to his groin.

"Did I get it?"

"No." He smiled. "You smeared it a little. Here." Again he glided his finger over her lips, then sucked that finger into his own mouth.

Her eyes were glued to him. "Oh," she breathed softly.

Yeah, oh. Traffic rushed all around them, and they sat there in their own little world. He had to get to the airport, and yet he didn't get back up. Instead, he leaned in so that their mouths were only a breath apart. "Let me get that last little bit—"

"Where—" Her tongue darted out, attempting to lick the chocolate off. "There?"

He smiled. "No."

She licked it again. "Now?"

"No."

"Dammit, Jacob."

"That's Mr. Wrong, to you." And still holding her face, he dropped his gaze from hers to look at her mouth, absorbing her little murmur of anticipation before he closed the gap and kissed her.

Chapter 6

It was the sugar rush, Maggie told herself. That, combined with the feel of Jacob pressed up against her again, and the warmth of his mouth . . . God. This was all his fault for being such a good kisser, all his fault, she thought as she pulled him even closer.

His reaction was an immediate approving rumble from deep in his chest and a tightening of his arms. So she hugged him tighter and gave him some tongue.

Hauling her into his lap with a groan, he kissed her long and hard and wet right there in the parking lot, until her entire body shivered in delight and anticipation.

She knew what he could do for her now, to her, and that made the longing worse. Given the sound he made, and how deliciously hard he'd gotten, he felt the same. The thrill of that surged through her. This big, bad, gorgeous man had already had her and *still* wanted her.

She felt drunk on the knowledge. Or it might have been the sugar. Either way, he had one arm around her, the other on her jaw, holding her face for his kiss; but then he pulled back, let out an unsteady breath and a short laugh. "There's no door to lock this time." He rose and offered her a hand, turning to her car. "Uh-oh. What happened to your tire?"

"It got a flat."

He crouched down next to it. "Yes, because someone slashed it." He took a careful look around them before cutting his no-longer-heated eyes to hers. "How long were you sitting here alone before I came?

"Wait. *Slashed?*" She took a closer look. "Do you think it was random?"

"Slashed tire seems pretty personal. You annoy anyone lately?"

"I annoy a lot of people. It's part of my charming nature." Spooked, she just stared at him. Her brain didn't feel like it was getting enough oxygen, so she decided to sit. Her tire had been slashed. Merry Christmas to her.

Ah, hell. Jacob looked over Maggie's head to where his truck was parked, complete with a plane ticket sitting on the front seat.

But he wasn't going anywhere.

And not just because his heart rate was still affected by that kiss, or because Maggie's lush mouth was still wet from his and he wanted to see what else was wet, but because he had a bad feeling that this smart, adorable, sexy woman who was nothing but trouble was *in* trouble. "Do you have a spare?"

"Yes." Her voice was muffled, but then she lifted her head. "And I took a class on how to change it, too."

Of course she had. He had a feeling this careful, organized, brilliant, sexy mess could do anything she set her mind to.

"Is it hot?" she asked. "I feel hot. Maybe it's nerves."

"It's not hot. It's actually chilly."

"Did you know that minus forty degrees Celsius is exactly the same as minus forty degrees Fahrenheit?"

"That's a new one for me." Knowing she was about to lose

it, he took her hand. "Listen, how about I change the tire for you, while you call the police and make a report."

"What if it's just one of the twenty-two percent of random, senseless acts of violence that people face in their lifetime?"

He slid her a glance. "You know, you'd really kick ass on *Jeopardy.*"

"I already did. That's how I paid for my PhD."

He shook his head in admiration as he pulled out his cell phone and called the police himself, but due to a high volume of calls, they wouldn't even come out and take a report.

"It's okay." Maggie pulled out her keys. "I'll just get the spare—Uh-oh," she said when she opened the trunk.

"Uh-oh?" He peered over her shoulder and saw nothing but stacks of craft supplies. "Where's your spare?"

"My sister borrowed my car. She's been volunteering at her kids' school, and my trunk is bigger than hers. She must have taken out the spare." She sighed. "Dammit. I'll call her."

"How about I just take you home?"

She lifted her gaze to his, her eyes still soft and heated, her cheeks flushed. "I don't know."

"You're not spooked at having your tire slashed but you're spooked at me driving you home?"

"Of course not." She gnawed her cheek a moment. "It's just that if we go to my house . . ."

He liked where that sentence was going. "Yeah?"

"Nothing. A ride would be great, thank you."

She squirmed all the way to her place in the Glendale Hills above L.A., her brain working so hard he could practically hear the wheels whirling. He pulled into the gated complex of her condo unit and looked at her. "Maggie."

She jumped. "Yes?"

"You do know this was just a ride, right?"

Her face flushed. "Of course. Just because we . . ."

"Had sex."

She winced. "Yes, that. Which doesn't mean we're going to pull off all our clothes and have *more* sex."

"Do you want to?"

She stared at him. "It was just a one-time thing." She seemed to hold her breath. "Right?"

He stroked a strand of hair along her temple. "It's whatever we want it to be. What do you want it to be, Maggie?"

"That's sort of the problem," she whispered. "I didn't think this far ahead, which is really unlike me."

"You like to think ahead."

"I really do."

"Okay, you go ahead and think on it then." He walked her to her door, where she turned to face him, pressing her spine up against the wood. "Thanks so much for the ride, but you don't have to come in."

"I want to. I want to make sure you're okay."

"Why wouldn't I be?"

"Because someone slashed your tire."

"That was random."

"Okay, but if I promise not to look at you even if you do strip your clothes off, can I please come in and make sure everything's okay?"

"You wouldn't look?" She looked intrigued at this. "Really?"

"Not if you didn't want me to."

"Oh." She looked so crestfallen, he laughed, and unable to help himself, he put his hands on her hips and pulled her in. "If you begged me," he murmured in her ear. "Maybe I'd look then."

She smiled, and it obliterated a few million of her brain cells.

"Okay, truth," he said. "I'd look. I'd look for a long time, and then I'd touch."

"Oh," she breathed, sounding a little turned on. "Really?"

"And then I'd taste. I'd lick and nibble and—"

The sound of glass shattering broke the night's silence. "What was that?" he asked.

"I don't know." She pulled out her keys and unlocked her front door, looking up at him questioningly when he held her back so he could enter first.

Her condo was dark, but enough of the streetlights shined in through the windows that he could see the living room was empty, and so was the kitchen. But the sliding glass door between the two, leading out onto a deck, was wide open to the night. "Did you leave the door like that?"

"No. No way."

Which, given her anal tendencies, he believed without question. He ran to the glass and looked out, where he could see a tipped-over ceramic bowl and plant—the source of the noise they'd heard.

Someone had just left, in a big hurry. He glanced down, saw the broken lock and moved to the edge of the deck, leaning over to see the path that lined the entire complex, which was well lit both ways for as far as he could see. There wasn't a single soul.

Her mysterious visitor had vanished.

He turned around and went back inside, where Maggie was turning on lights in the living room, revealing soft, muted beachy colors and a neat, minimalist style. He pulled out his cell phone to call the police. "Is anything missing?"

"No."

He spoke to dispatch, was assured a car would come out to investigate, and slipped his phone into his pocket. He eyed the couch and matching chair, the coffee table, all perfectly arranged and perfectly neat. Much like the woman. "Let's check upstairs."

The minimalist trend continued on the second floor, with one big exception—her bathroom. While he stood in the doorway, mouth open, enthralled by the sight, she was hastily yanking down a forest of hanging lingerie. Yellow silk, blue satin, black lace, a virtual cornucopia of exoticness that made thinking all but impossible.

"Don't look!" she demanded, shoving everything in a small drawer. She pulled at a simple white cotton thong that was maybe two square inches of material. "You're still looking!" She was all breathless and adorably sexy, and desperate to hide her things. "Close your eyes!"

"I'm sorry," he said with a laugh, when she twisted to glare at him. "I can't hear a word you're saying, you just blew all my remaining brain cells. Do you really wear all this . . . ?" He fingered a set of garters, black silk, and felt himself get hard.

"Yes." She yanked it out of his fingers and shoved it into one of her pockets. "Lots of women wear pretty things beneath their clothes, you know. It's not like I'm a freak."

"Oh, baby, I never thought you were a freak." He put his hands on her arms and halted her frenetic movements. "That's not what I was thinking at all."

"What are you thinking?" she whispered.

He looked into her beautiful face and those eyes that had a way of sneaking past all his defenses. "I'm thinking you're the smartest, funniest, most fascinating woman I've ever met. And you're so desperate to hide your sexy garters that I'm wondering what else you're hiding."

She ignored that. "Fascinating is a euphemism. You might as well say I have a good personality."

"You do."

"We both know what it means when someone says that. It means I'm a dog."

At that, he tossed back his head and laughed.

"That's funny?"

"Yes." He hugged her from behind, turning them so that she faced the bathroom mirror. She had a baby blue bra in one hand and sea green panties in her other. Her hair was its usual rioted, gorgeous mess, and her face . . . Good God, she had a face that reached out and slayed his heart. "You're beautiful," he said, meeting her eyes in the mirror. "So goddamned beautiful, you take my breath away."

She dropped the lingerie. Twisting in his arms until she faced him, she cupped his face. "You're beautiful, too. I know you're not supposed to tell a guy that, but it's true. And I don't mean just on the outside." She sighed. "I'm sorry I ate all the cookies I made you, and I'm sorry I needed a ride home. You should go, I know you have a flight."

Had a flight. "Are you sorry you chose me as your Mr. Wrong?"

"No." Her gaze dropped to his mouth. "Do you think it was a fluke? You know, how good it was between us?"

He arched a brow. "A fluke?"

"Yeah. Maybe . . . maybe we should do it again. Just to make sure, you know?"

Suddenly the blood was rushing from his head for parts south. He nodded, and in the interest of getting to the "again"—which hopefully would involve some of that hot as hell lingerie, he leaned in. He'd just touched his mouth to hers, body hot and hard and ready, when from down below, her doorbell rang.

The police had arrived.

"Maybe we can pretend we don't hear them," she whispered against his lips, all flushed and heated and sweet, sexy acquiescence in his arms.

He was all for that idea, but unfortunately the police weren't going to be ignored. The doorbell rang again, and with a sigh, she backed out of his arms and headed out of the bathroom, the black garters sticking out of her pocket.

Chapter 7

The police took a report, but with nothing missing, nothing even out of place other than the broken lock, they didn't seem too hopeful on getting Maggie answers anytime soon.

When they were gone, she settled back against the front door and eyed the big, bad, sexy man standing in the middle of her living room. "Thanks for staying," she said, her hormones much more firmly in control now that he wasn't touching her. "I'll be fine."

He came close. His hands settled on the wood on either side of her face as he leaned in. He smelled like her idea of heaven, and looked good enough to eat—better than even her cookies.

"Will you?" he murmured.

"Absolutely. Maybe you can still catch your flight."

"That ship has sailed." He was so close that his body heat seeped into her bones, so close that she could feel that there wasn't an ounce of softness to him, anywhere. "Back to our other conversation. So, Maggie Bell, what other secrets are you hiding?" He tilted his head, letting the tip of his nose glide along her jawline.

Oh, God. What was she hiding? Nothing. Nothing at all. Well, except that she'd apparently renewed her huge crush . . .

He came in even closer, and opened his mouth on her earlobe, making her eyes cross with lust.

"D-did you know that Kansas state law requires pedestrians crossing the highways at night to wear taillights?" she stammered.

"I didn't. But what I do want to know is, how come you've denied your body pleasure for two years?"

"*Nearly* two years," she corrected, and felt him smile against her skin. "And I haven't completely denied myself. I have a showerhead."

He laughed silkily and she bit her lip to keep any more ridiculous admissions from escaping, sucking in desperately needed air as he glided his mouth along her jaw to her throat. She was melting into a boneless puddle of longing when the doorbell rang again—making her nearly jump out of her skin. Pushing him aside, she ran down the stairs and opened the door to . . .

"Scott," she said, in surprise. She heard Jacob come into the entryway and stop just on the other side of the door, not visible to Scott. Behind the door, she put her hand on his chest to hold him there.

"I saw your car in the lot," Scott told her. "But you weren't in the building anywhere. I got worried. Your tire—"

"I know." Funny how just looking at him had always made her a little dizzy from all his fabulousness, but now she didn't want to look at him.

She wanted to look at Jacob. Jacob, whose warm chest was pushing back just a little against her palm.

"I called our mechanic for you. It'll be fixed by morning," Scott said. "But how did you get home?"

She leaned into the door, trapping Jacob between the wall and the door. "I thought you were already gone. I thought everyone was gone. A friend brought me here. Thank you for calling your mechanic."

"No problem." He was looking past her, as if hoping he'd get invited in, and also trying to see the "friend." The friend who with shocking stealth filched the garters right out of her pocket, the thief.

"So who slashed your tire?" Scott asked.

"Probably just a random thing. Well . . ." She flashed a quick smile. "Thanks for coming by—" She tried to shut the door but he put a hand on it.

"Want to grab dinner?"

How long had she imagined this, him asking her out, then having her realize she was the woman of his dreams? But then, she'd been with Jacob and now . . . and now she couldn't imagine being with Scott at all. "Actually, Scott, I'm—"

"Trying to figure out who might have broken into her house."

Maggie turned her head and locked gazes with Jacob, who smiled sweetly—*sweetly?*—as he came out from the other side of the door, standing a little close as he smiled politely at Scott.

Scott blinked. "Jacob? What are you doing here? And break-in? Here? Was anything stolen?"

Jacob narrowed his eyes. "Usually the first question is, are you okay?"

"Of course, of course." Scott slapped his forehead. "I'm just flustered. A slashed tire and now a break-in. And you . . . you visiting. Maggie, are you okay?"

Well, let's see. She had Jacob—who now had her garters in his pocket—on one side, and Scott, her maybe Mr. Right—who was currently eyeing Jacob—on the other.

Who was eyeing Scott right back.

Two men. Both wanting her. "I'm fine."

"Maybe you should come back with me until we know you're safe."

"I'm staying," Jacob said casually. "She'll be safe."

The testosterone level in the air rose to dangerous heights.

"I could stay, too," Scott said. "No problem."

Oh, yes, it was a problem. They were *both* a problem. And she had no experience with which to deal with this. She needed Janie. "Okay," she said, gently pushing Scott over the threshold. "Thank you very much for coming by, but I'm going to be fine."

Jacob smirked.

So she shoved *him* over the threshold as well. "And you have a flight to catch."

"But—"

"Good night," she said, firmly. "To the both of you." She shut the door, letting out a slow, shaky breath as she leaned back against the wood, suddenly thankful she had Mr. Showerhead after all.

She ate a can of soup and a piece of toast, and didn't let herself think about the nice dinner Scott might have taken her to. Or what she might be doing with Jacob right now if Scott hadn't interrupted them. She changed into her pj's and slathered on some of her skin care from the vial.

Someone knocked at her door and she hesitated, then looked through the peephole.

A dark eye looked back at her. A dark eye that seemed to be filled with both wry humor and annoyance, complete with a dash of affection.

Jacob pulled back so that she could see all six-feet-two inches of his leanly muscled frame, the one that tended to make her brain cells simultaneously combust.

He waggled his fingers at her.

She pressed her forehead to the door while her heart went off like a jackhammer. "Go away, Jacob."

"Let me in."

Just his voice made her quiver. What was wrong with her?

"Stress," he said through the wood when she inadvertently spoke out loud. "That's what's wrong. I have the cure for that, by the way."

Oh, God. "Stressed is desserts spelled backward." She could use a dessert right about now. . . .

Then he did something to really turn her on. He lifted a bag of chocolate cookies to the peephole. "Cookies that you don't have to make. And unlike someone I know, I didn't eat them all. Open up, Maggie."

With a sigh, she grabbed a throw blanket from her couch and threw it around her. "I'm in my pj's."

"I won't look."

A reluctant smile tugged at her mouth, and she pulled open the door. He was wearing clean clothes: a pair of dark Levi's, a dark polo shirt, and a dark smile to match, which had her pulse leaping to attention.

Bad pulse. "I don't need you to stay—"

"I know." He pushed past her and tossed a duffel bag down to her couch. "But I am."

He smelled good. Dammit, why did he always have to smell good?

She put her hands on her hips. "Jacob—"

Turning back to her, he gripped her waist, pulled her up against him and kissed her until she didn't know her name. Disarmed, she stared up at him when he pulled back. "What does that have to do with anything?"

"It has to do with the fact that I wouldn't leave you alone tonight even if I didn't want to do *that* all the damn time." He shoved his fingers through his hair and turned in a slow circle, coming back to face her, his eyes dark and full of things that took her breath. "Look, you were there for me once. Let me be here for you now. Don't ask me to leave you alone tonight."

She thought about how she'd felt earlier standing between him and Scott, how really, there hadn't been any choice to make at all. And how that scared her because she no longer understood herself or what she wanted. "We're not having sex."

"Let me guess. Because you have your showerhead."

She'd known that would come back and bite her on the ass.

"Don't worry, I understand. I doubt any guy could compete with a showerhead. How about a blanket? Can I ask for a blanket?"

She pulled one out from the small chest she used as an ottoman, then watched him kick off his shoes and lie down on her couch. He was of course too long for it, with his calves and feet sticking off the end, but he merely tossed the blanket over himself and closed his eyes. "Could you get the light?"

She just stared at him. "You missed your flight for me. Why did you miss your flight for me?"

"I realize you've been using a showerhead as a boyfriend, so you might have forgotten how the friend part works. Friends stick by each other when they're in trouble."

"We're friends?"

"Well, we're not sleeping together."

He said this a little irritably, which made her want to smile. "I'm not in trouble, Jacob."

"I think you're mistaken. Go to sleep, Maggie. I'm exhausted, far too exhausted to argue with you. Maybe even too exhausted to have all that sex you don't want to have."

She turned off the light. "Is there anything else you need?"

"Probably you should be more specific."

There in the dark, she both rolled her eyes and felt . . . hungry. "Good night."

" 'Night."

She went to bed, and fell sleep while trying to remember why they weren't having sex. *Just a one-time thing,* she reminded herself . . . and woke up in the middle of the night dying of thirst. Or at least that was the excuse she gave herself for wanting to steal a peek at the gorgeous man sleeping over. She tiptoed into the living room and found him sprawled on her couch, both legs hanging off, one arm dangling down, face relaxed, chest rising and falling in a slow rhythm.

He wasn't a snorer. Good to know. God, she really wished she'd asked for a *two*-time thing instead of a one-time thing. If he opened his eyes right now, she'd just tell him so.

But he didn't.

She shuffled her feet. Cleared her throat.

He still didn't budge.

Dammit. Stepping closer, she touched his blanket. Faked a sneeze. *Nothing.* Feeling like an idiot, she went to the kitchen. There were no clean glasses in the cupboard, but her dishwasher was clean so she grabbed one from there. Then she opened the refrigerator door for something to drink, and in the harsh glare of the refrigerator light, caught a glimpse of movement on her right.

Her intruder. Without thinking, she shoved the refrigerator door into him, hearing the "oomph" of air leaving a set of lungs.

Irrational fear took over, and she backed up, tripping over the open dishwasher, which she fell into, hitting her butt on the still open bottom tray, *hard.* The whole thing gave, falling out of its hinges, hitting the floor, taking her down with it.

"Maggie!" At the crashing sound, Jacob slapped his hands along the wall, looking for the light.

"Don't turn on the light!" she cried.

Okay, she was alive, but he could hear the pain in her voice. Although *he* was the one who'd been hit in the belly with a refrigerator . . .

He'd been asleep for maybe an hour before the sheer discomfort of the short sofa had gotten to him. That and the soft padded footsteps of Maggie leaving her bedroom. When she'd stood over him, he'd held his breath rather than say anything, because what would have come out of his mouth would have been "I like your pj's, now take them off." Then she'd gone into the kitchen, and he had no idea why, but he'd followed without saying a word, which turned out to be a mistake because she'd slammed the refrigerator door into his gut.

Finally, he found a light switch and hit it, and then went still as he took in the sight.

"I told you not to," Maggie said on a sigh.

She was sitting in the opened dishwasher tray in a camisole and panty set, bare legs dangling over the sides, her arms bracing her up as she attempted to lever herself off the broken plates beneath her. "Jesus, Maggie." She had to be cut all to hell, and he rushed forward to lift her out.

But she held him off. "Don't touch me." She tried to lift herself out and failed. "Okay, touch me."

Yeah. He just wished she meant it.

Chapter 8

"I'm fine!" Maggie shouted this for the third time in as many minutes through her bedroom door to a worried-sounding Jacob.

How she'd managed to lift herself off of the broken plates and glasses—and let's not forget the utensils—she hardly knew. She'd managed only with Jacob's help, as if the whole situation hadn't been embarrassing enough, and then she'd escaped down the hall and into her bedroom.

The mirror over her dresser wasn't telling her much so she moved into her bathroom, stood on the toilet to get onto the counter, pulled down her panties, and twisted around to look into the vanity mirror.

Not good. She had a few cuts oozing a little blood, and already bruises were blooming. Nothing appearing too serious, but they weren't pretty. At the knock on her bedroom door, she nearly fell off the counter. "Don't come in!"

"Maggie, let me see."

"No!"

"You've got to be cut up. There's blood in the dishwasher."

Ew.

"You might have glass splinters."

Oh, no, she did not. She poked at one of the cuts, sucked in a harsh breath of pain, and admitted he might be right. But if she did have glass in there, it was staying in there.

Forever.

Jacob knocked one more time, didn't get an answer, and thought *fuck it.* He opened her bedroom door.

He had a quick view of the four-poster iron-rod bed piled high with pillows and thick bedding before he turned to the open bathroom door.

She was standing on the counter yanking up her panties, where she'd clearly been trying to get an up close and personal view of her injuries.

"Hey! The bedroom door was shut!"

"And I opened it." He strode over to her, scooped her up off the counter and put her down, accidentally knocking her toothbrush to the floor. "How bad is it?"

She slid her hands to her ass. "Not bad at all."

"Liar." He picked up her toothbrush and put it back on the counter, but she shook her head. "Wrong side."

"Huh?"

"That's the toilet side of the counter. Dentists recommend that a toothbrush be kept at least six feet away from the toilet to avoid airborne particles resulting from the flush. You just put it within four feet. I'll have to throw it away."

"I'll buy you a new one. Enough stalling. Let me see."

Resignation flashed across her face, as well as discomfort at the realization he saw right through her. "No," she said.

"This isn't the time for modesty, Maggie."

"I'm fine."

Uh-huh. And he was the damn tooth fairy. He peeked around her to catch sight of her in the mirror. The back of her camisole dipped low, revealing her shoulders and spine, lovely and smooth. And as he already knew, the panties were small, boy cut, and revealed more lovely, smooth skin. They rode low on her hips, yet slid up high enough to reveal the bottom curve of her sweet ass. She was holding said sweet ass but he could still see that one cheek was bleeding. "You're not fine."

She sagged, letting her shoulders fall as she dropped her gaze from his and pulled out a box of Band-Aids. "Okay, dammit, I'm not."

All irritation vanished. "Come on," he said gently, and grabbing the box of Band-Aids, pulled her into her bedroom. "You should really buy stock in these." He sat on the bed and patted the mattress next to him.

Miserably, she shook her head. "I can't sit."

"Lie down."

"Oh, God," she moaned, still holding her butt. "I should have just stayed sleeping. Did you know that we burn more calories sleeping than we do watching TV?"

"Fascinating. Come on, it won't be that bad."

"That's because it's not you baring *your* ass."

"True." He patted the mattress again. "How about I close one eye, will that help?"

She let out a low, glum laugh, and crawled up on the bed. "Did you know that elephants are the only animals with four knees?"

"I did not know that." He was trying not to know other things. Like she possibly had the sweetest ass he'd ever seen.

Slowly, carefully, she sprawled out on her tummy. "Did you know that every human spent about a half hour as a single cell?"

"Maggie, don't be nervous."

"Or that every year about ninety-eight percent of the atoms in your body are replaced?"

"Fascinating. Listen, it's going to be okay, I promise." One spaghetti strap of her cami had slid down over her arm. The hem had risen to mid-back, revealing a strip of skin that he wanted to nibble. Her legs and feet were bare. He wanted to start at her toes and lick his way up to the world-class wedgie she had going on.

"Jacob?"

He cleared his throat. The last time a woman had lain on her belly for him, he'd been naked and about to have a very different experience. "Yeah?"

"Just look already!"

"Okay." He very gently slid the material of her panties over one cheek, so that it further bunched in the middle. Her entire body was clenched so tight, she quivered. "Relax," he said, stroking his finger over the already blooming bruise.

She let out a sound that might have been a laugh. "You pull down your pants and we'll see if you can relax. What do you see?"

He saw two creamy cheeks that were so perfect he wanted to lean down and kiss them, divided by the bunched-up silk that much to his regret managed to hide all the feminine secrets between her thighs.

"Jacob!"

Right. What did he see? Since she didn't want to hear that he saw things that made him weak in the knees, he cleared his throat. "You're already bruising and need ice."

She wriggled around. "Any glass?"

"Hold still." She had two long cuts from the broken plate. He probed them both while she hissed out a breath. "No glass," he finally said, reaching for the Band-Aids. "All you need is a little TLC. . . ." He covered the wounds and then, because he couldn't seem to help himself, he bent over her and did as he'd been dying to, and kissed the spot.

She gasped and rolled painfully to her side, her hair in her face, her eyes wide. "What was that?"

"I was kissing it all better. Did it work?"

"I . . ." She blinked and slid her hands beneath her to cup her bottom. "Yeah."

Both cami straps had slipped down now. Her breasts were full, pressing against the thin material, her nipples two hard, mouthwatering points. Her gently curved belly was rising and falling with each breath, of which she took many. Her panties were snug, the effect being that the satin did little more than outline her every dip and nuance, and if he thought he'd wanted to nibble her ass, it was nothing compared with this particular area.

"Jacob?"

With difficulty, he lifted his gaze to her face.

"You really are different," she whispered.

"From . . . ?"

"Me."

That tugged a laugh out of him. "Yeah, and trust me, I'm very grateful for those differences."

"No, it's just that you were right before. The guys I usually fall for are the male version of me."

He paused as that sank in. "Are you falling for me, Maggie?"

Now it was her turn to pause. "I didn't think it would be possible."

"Because we're so different."

"That's right."

He felt himself go very still. Shit, he'd really been an idiot. Standing, he walked out of the bedroom, away from the gorgeous creature in silk, so he could think a moment. And what he thought made him very unhappy. All the alluding to Mr. Right and Mr. Wrong, the times she'd mentioned their differences . . . While he'd been enjoying those differences, *she'd* been thinking he was a step down for her. A big step. How it'd never occurred to him, he had no idea, but—

"Jacob."

She'd followed him into the living room. He let out a breath and stared out her window into the dark night. "I realize I don't have the fancy degrees or the high-paying job, but I don't like the idea that you're just slumming with me."

"No. No, you misunderstood. We're different, yes. As in I'm anal, single-minded to the point of obsession, and frankly, socially handicapped."

He turned to face her but she held up a hand before he could speak. "You, however . . ." she continued softly, "you're tough and confident and funny and effortlessly sexy. I've never been with a guy like you, Jacob, and now I know I short-changed myself. That's what I meant before. Yes, I've been interested in you since I first saw you again on your ladder in a pair of worn Levi's, looking in charge of your world, and yeah, that's extremely shallow of me, but it's so much more than that. I love the way you think, how you always say what you mean, no guesswork. What you see is what you get with you, and that's . . ." She searched for the words. "Incredibly appealing."

"I've been interested in you since I first saw you again," he said. "Before I even knew it was *again*."

She looked surprised. "Really?"

"Yeah, really. You were wearing a black skirt and a white blouse, with a peekaboo hint of lace beneath. And fuck-me heels."

She choked out a laugh. "I was not. They were higher than my usual, but I had a meeting that day and was looking for power."

"You got lust."

"My hair was out of control."

"It was up in some complicated twist and you had a few strands of hair falling out the back, dangling against your sweet neck. You were late, you were rushing, and you looked like a hot mess. Emphasis on the hot. But even then it was your brain that attracted me most. I love watching you think, Maggie."

"Do you know what I'm thinking now?" She stepped closer and slid her hands up his chest. Wrapping her arms around his neck, she pressed all that hotness up against him.

"I could guess," he murmured.

She smiled, and it staggered him. "My life has always been MapQuested out," she whispered. "The route carefully highlighted. But with you, I don't know what to expect, I don't know what you're thinking or what you're going to do. Nothing is planned out, nothing is guaranteed, and it's . . . exciting, Jacob."

His hand swept down her body and up again. "So I turn your body on."

"You turn my head on." She caught his face in her hands and went up on tiptoe. He could feel her breasts, nipples hard, pressing into his chest. "Do you understand?" she murmured against his mouth. "This isn't a fifth date, where I've carefully reflected and decided it's time to put 'have sex' on the calendar. I haven't lit a candle or turned on the music like I usually do because that's what sets the mood and helps me relax. I haven't slathered myself in some pretty-scented lotion to make sure I'm turning you on. Hell, I didn't shave my legs—" She went still and closed her eyes, relaxing back down on the balls of her feet. "Dammit, I didn't shave my legs."

He grabbed her before she could turn away, hauling her back up against him. "I don't care. Finish. Finish what you were going to say."

"I want you because you're different from the norm for me. I want you because when I'm with you, I don't have to think. I can just feel. I know we said this was a one-time thing, but make me feel again, Jacob, just once more." She stepped back, then slowly slid first one spaghetti strap off her shoulder, and then the other, letting the cami slip. It snagged on her nipples for one heart-stopping second, then fell, revealing her mouth-watering breasts. She nudged it past her hips, where it landed in a puddle of silk at her feet. Eyes on his, she hooked her fingers in her panties, and he stopped breathing. "Love me, Jacob," she whispered, gliding them down past her injuries—which made her want to wince, he could tell—past her thighs to join the cami at her feet. Straightening, she reached for his shirt. "Love me."

He had a feeling he already did, but that wasn't what she meant, and all she wanted from him was this adventure, was what he could do to her in bed, so he tugged his shirt off over his head, lifted her up, and carried her back to her bedroom.

Maggie expected Jacob to put her on the bed and then fol-low her down, but instead he sat on the mattress with her in his lap, his spine against the headboard.

"So you don't put your weight on your cuts," he said, pulling her thighs on either side of his hips so that she straddled him, letting her feel exactly what her kisses and touches had done to him.

There was something about being entirely naked while he still wore his jeans. It made her feel exposed, and yet so aroused she could hardly stand it. "I'm a little underdressed here."

"I know." His eyes were lit with heat and desire as they took her naked body in. "I like it." Then he covered her mouth with his, going in for a long, drugging kiss that did something shocking to her brain that she'd never managed before.

It turned off.

She wasn't worried about what she looked like naked, or wondering if she'd turned off her cell phone, or if her front door was locked. She wasn't doing anything but feeling—and oh, God, what a feeling she had with his hands skimming down her bare back, cupping her bottom, gently pulling her in closer, careful of her cuts and bruises, until she was as snug against him as she could be, making her intimately aware of his jeans. The denim rubbed her inner thighs, and between.

He was hard. Big and hard and she pulled her mouth free to pop open his buttons, while his hands stroked her breasts, gliding over her nipples, leaving her to restlessly rock her hips. "Jacob—"

"I know." He took his hands on a tour down her ribs, her quivering belly, her thighs, which he urged even wider. His gaze dropped from hers, and he looked his fill, exhaling very heavily, very slowly, only to suck the air back in when she freed him from his jeans. Lifting his hips, he helped her shove them out of the way as his hands swept up her back, pulling her in close for another deep, soul-wrenching kiss, his hands making their way back down, over her bandages, between her legs. "God, you're wet. So wet. I want to taste—"

"Later—" She gasped out the word as he slid a finger into her. Needing him inside her, she lifted her hips.

"Wait," he rasped out. "Maggie, wait. I want to—"

She sank onto him, and he gripped her hips to hold her still, his eyes trapping hers. Their twin sighs commingled in the air, and she knew right then, nothing about this was a one-time fluke.

"Maggie," he said, just that. She rocked her hips to meet his, staring with wide wonder into his eyes, her hands touching as much of his hard, damp, straining body as she could. Yeah, it'd been a while, a long while since she'd been with anyone else, and yet she could say with the utmost authority that it had *never* felt like this.

And then he began to move. Her toes curled, her entire body tingled from the inside out as sheer, unadulterated pleasure hummed through her. It was perfect, it was heaven, and when he banded his arms tightly around her, pushing up, thrusting hard, his teeth scraping her throat, she felt herself start to come apart for him again.

But this time, he was right there with her, just as far gone himself, and when she came on a cry of sheer surprise at the infusion of pleasure, she heard his own low, rough groan as he shuddered and followed her over.

Chapter 9

Jacob woke up to a knock, and opened his eyes. Plastered against his side was a soft, naked, sleeping woman with a smile on her face that said *I'm in an orgasmic coma.*

He'd put her there, which gave him more than a little satisfaction. With a smile, he leaned over her with the intention of waking her up and starting all over again but then he heard another knock and realized someone was at the door. Maggie didn't budge, so he slipped out of bed. At the loss of his body heat, she rolled to her belly and snuggled into her pillow—with two Band-Aids on her cute ass, and a bruise in the shape of a fork.

Someone knocked for a third time and he pulled on his jeans, padded through the condo, and opened the front door.

Scott stared at Jacob for a long beat, holding two Starbucks cups and a brown bag that smelled good. He took in Jacob's lack of a shirt and shoes and socks, and clearly added two and two. "Uh . . ."

"You're looking for Maggie."

Scott nodded, looking very unhappy. "Yes."

"She's still in bed—"

"No, I'm here." Maggie came around from behind him, wearing a robe and a wide-eyed, sexy, rumpled, I've-just-been-laid look in spite of how tightly she held her robe closed. "Scott?"

He held out one of the coffees, and then on second thought, politely handed the other to Jacob. "I came by to check in on you, but I can see you're . . . busy."

"Scott—"

"No, it's okay. See you at work." With a smile that didn't reach his eyes, he turned and walked off.

"Scott."

He didn't respond, and shutting the door, Maggie leaned back against it and sighed. "That's probably not good."

"Actually, it is." Jacob took a second sip. "For how overpriced it is, it's very good."

Maggie didn't smile. "You didn't have to act so . . ."

"So what?"

"Territorial."

That stopped him cold. Territorial? He wasn't territorial. Territorial was for committed guys, guys who had a thing for being with the same woman, guys who wanted stability and routine—not guys just being a woman's Mr. Wrong. He was just . . . ah, hell. *He was acting territorial.* While he chewed on that shocking fact, she made a noise of disgust and brushed past him, heading into the shower. She'd just shut the curtain when he caught up with her and peeled back the shower curtain.

With a squeak, she tried to cover herself up.

"I've already seen it all." He stepped out of his jeans and into the shower with her, crowding her back against the tile.

"Jacob."

"Maggie." He dropped his attitude and set his forehead to hers. "Truth. I guess I am feeling . . . territorial."

She was no longer covering herself up but looking at him with a rather complimentary wide-eyed wonder. "Are we going to—"

"Oh, yeah. We're going to."

When Maggie finally got to work, thanks to a ride from Janie, she'd had two more orgasms and had completely revised her opinion of the dreaded "morning after." In fact, she grinned all the way into the building, was *still* grinning when she passed by Alice's desk.

Alice took one look at her face and swore. "Are you kidding me? *You* got laid? I can't get a freaking return phone call from my supposed boyfriend and you, of the Church of Chemistry, got laid?"

Maggie looked around to make sure no one was listening. "How can you tell?"

"I know Scott went by your place last night, and you look all loose and relaxed. Two scientist geeks doing the nasty." Alice sighed. "Some people have all the luck."

"I didn't sleep with Scott."

"No sleeping, huh? Sure. Rub it in."

"Alice," Maggie said on a laugh. "I didn't have sex with Scott."

"Hey, you don't want to dish. I get it. You don't know me all that well, and—"

"No, it's not that—" She broke off as Jacob walked down the hall. He looked . . . different. And it wasn't just because she'd seen his big, bad body in the buff now, had in fact nibbled her way up and down every inch of that six-foot-two frame.

He didn't look like the Jacob she'd seen every day for two months. He wasn't wearing his tool belt, or his jeans, but a pair of nice-fitting cargoes and a white button-down. If he put on a white lab coat, he'd look every bit as much the on-the-go professional as any of the guys in this building. In fact, suddenly he looked like . . . like her Mr. Right, which should have been thrilling, but oddly enough it didn't matter. Because sexy and gorgeous as he was, it happened to be what was on the inside that attracted her. He made her smile, he made her think, he made her feel like so much more than the sum of her chemistry degrees—he made her feel like a warm, sexy woman.

Somehow, in some way, her Mr. Wrong had become her Mr. Right.

"Ohmigod," Alice whispered, dividing a stare between Maggie and Jacob. "*Him?* You slept with him?"

Maggie gave a guilty little start. "I have no idea what you're talking about."

Alice laughed. "Oh, yes, you do." She watched Jacob walk toward them. "So was he as hot as he looks?"

Maggie bit her lip, and Alice shook her head. "You don't have to say a word, your face is saying it all for you. So you two are what, dating now?"

"No. It was . . . a one-time thing." Okay, *two* . . .

"Well, that's just a damn shame."

Jacob came to a stop in front of Maggie. As if he couldn't care less that there were people milling around, not to mention Alice staring at him with open curiosity. He leaned in and gave Maggie a kiss. "Hi."

"Hi." She was breathless. He'd given her a peck and she couldn't breathe.

Oh, and her nipples were hard.

But it was more than that. Just looking at him had her heart tipping over on its side and exposing its tender underbelly. Oh, no. She'd fallen for him and couldn't get up. . . .

"You okay?" he asked.

No. No, she wasn't. She shifted away from Alice's desk for privacy, pulling him with her. "What are you doing here?"

"I wanted to say good-bye before I got on the plane. And make sure that you stay with your sister the next few nights."

"I will, but I'll be okay."

"I know. But I didn't want to walk away without making sure."

Walk away. Damn, she'd nearly forgotten that part, which had been her own idea. "I hope you have a great holiday with your family."

He just looked at her for a long moment, saying nothing. Then finally he nodded, his eyes fathomless and unreadable. "Thanks. You, too."

"Maggie?" Alice called out, waving her back over. "Did you leave your office light on last night?"

"No, I—" She whipped around and saw the light gleaming from beneath the door. *Not again.* What the hell was going on? Pulling out her key, she let herself in and gasped. Her files, locked when she'd left yesterday, were all open and disheveled.

"So they got the chance to search this time," Jacob said, coming in behind her. "What are they looking for, your formula?"

"I'm not sure." There were only two people in this building besides herself who had keys to her office, she'd checked yesterday. Well, three. Alice, of course.

And Scott and Tim.

They'd been acting strange and just a little bit off all week now, and she'd ignored it. "Alice?"

"Yes?"

"Could you give us a minute?"

"Oh! Sure."

When she was gone, Maggie pulled the vial of her formula from her briefcase and turned to Jacob. "I think it's all connected to this." She slipped the vial into her pocket. "The slashed tire. My home intruder. The odd visits from Scott . . ."

The odd visits from Scott. *He* was behind this? *Why?* It made no sense at all. "Wait here. I'll be right back." Leaving him, she rushed down the hall and barged into Scott's office.

The room was large and plush, the desk and other furniture all inventions he'd sponsored. The desk was an alloy material that couldn't be scratched. The couch was one of the brand-new magnetic designs, a flat pad sitting on the floor now but when a switch on Scott's desk was hit, the cushion bent in half, providing back support, and floated off the floor, held there by the opposing magnets buried in the cushion. It wasn't activated because of the fatal flaw of the design—when switched on, everything in the room that was metal—the phone receiver, paper clips, letter openers—went flying rather violently through the air to stick to the couch. The inventor still had the scars to prove it.

Scott sat at the desk now, with three big-screen computer monitors going, one that looked like a patient monitor, revealing blood pressure, heart rate, pulse, etcetera. The second screen was a global positioning system, but before she could catch sight of the third, Scott looked up at her, jumped guiltily, and hit a button on his keyboard that shut everything down.

"What was all that?" she asked.

"Nothing. Just . . . work."

"Are you stalking me, Scott?"

"What?" He looked genuinely shocked. "Why would I stalk you?"

"I wish I knew. Someone's been in my office twice now, clearly looking for something. And then there's my tire. And someone in my condo. And you and Tim acting . . . weird."

"No. Not weird, I swear. And maybe Tim needed something—"

"My files were trashed, Scott. Maybe I should just call the police and let them sort it out."

"Okay, let's not get crazy here," he said, losing a little of the tan he'd bought himself. "I'm sure we can figure this out in-house. *I* can figure this out in-house, I'm sure of it."

She looked at his computer, wishing she could see what he'd been working on, what had made him jump so guiltily. "So you want me to . . ."

"Do nothing. I'll handle it. I'll check into it immediately and get back to you."

"I still think that the police—"

"Totally not necessary."

"Scott."

"Give me until noon, okay? Just a few hours, Maggie. If I don't have answers by then, you can go to the police. *We'll* go to the police."

"Fine. Noon." She walked out of his office, knowing that somehow she needed to get a look at his computer—alone.

Jacob found Maggie walking the hallway, lost in thought. "What are you doing?"

"The average person walks the equivalent of five times around the equator in their lifetime. I'm just doing my part."

"Maggie." She was clearly tense again, as she'd been before last night. He'd had great success at unwinding her then, getting her to relax, turning her into a pile of boneless jelly.

She'd done the same for him.

And that had been great, but it'd gone deeper for him. It'd always been deeper for him. Walking away was going to hurt, big-time, and yet that's what the plan had been.

She looked at him with those gorgeous, heart-and-soul eyes, and voiced his thoughts. "I know I said I wanted a one-time thing."

"Technically, it's been a three-time thing, at least for me. For you, it's been more like a six- or seven-time thing—"

"My point," she said, blushing, "is that I lied, and not just because I need your help now. I *do* need your help, but I just want you to know I lied because you scare me."

That was just convoluted enough to make sense, and he linked his fingers with hers. "Well, we're even there. You scare me too. How can I help, Maggie?"

She stared up at him, her heart in her eyes. "I need Scott pre-occupied for a few minutes so I can snoop on his computer. Any ideas?"

"Yes." He pulled out his cell and called the crane operator, who happened to be in the lot still loading his equipment. "Dan? I have a favor . . ."

Two minutes later, Scott got word his Mercedes was blocked in by a crane, and he went running out of the building.

Maggie helped herself into his office, locked the door behind her, and went immediately to his desk. One touch to the mouse had all the computer windows flickering to life. It took her a moment to grasp what she was seeing, and when she did, her heart stopped, then kicked back into gear when someone knocked.

"Maggie?"

At Jacob's voice, she ran to the door to let him in, then locked it again behind him.

"No one saw me," he said, looking around at the neat office, at the pad sitting on the floor. "What is that?"

"Magnetic couch. When you flip that switch on the desk, it floats in the air, but duck because anything metal in the room goes flying through the air. Look at this." She pointed to the screen. "Scott's been busy." One window had Maggie's picture and bio up, along with the stats and ingredients on her body cream, with the surprise and critical element Scott had alluded to, and it wasn't a thickening agent. The second window revealed a heart rate and pulse monitor. The third was the GPS system, with a grid map of the city, the highlighted portion blinking in on downtown, specifically Sixth Street. More specifically, this building.

Here.

As it all sank in, the heart rate and pulse monitored on the screen picked up speed, beeping, beeping, beeping in rhythm to her own.

"It's you," Jacob guessed, his voice low, calm, and furious.

"Yes."

"How? *Why?*"

Leaning forward, she clicked on the files just behind her picture and bio. "Scott and Tim added an ingredient to my lotion. They let me think it was a texturing element but they lied. It's atom-sized transmitting microchips. It's genius, really, if you think of the implications. A heart patient, for instance. With the micro-transmitters in place, it would assist doctors in treating their patients. You could change a dose without ever having to see the patient, or even just monitor someone from long distances, allow them to live their lives, calling them in only when they were in danger, or—"

"Maggie."

She broke off and sighed. "Okay, I know. Gross invasion of privacy."

"You think?"

"Yes, of course. Not to mention completely illegal. But why the secrecy? Why didn't they just tell me? It's amazing."

"Gee, I don't know, maybe because of the *illegal* part?"

"Well, there's that," Scott said, coming into his office, twirling his keys on his fingers. He saw the computer windows up and his mouth tightened. "And for what it's worth, I wanted to tell you all along."

Tim shoved him aside and came in behind him. "But I didn't. And as for the so-called stalking—about which, FYI, I prefer to use the word surveillance—we simply needed the vial back, before you figured out what we were up to."

"But you gave it to me," Maggie reminded him.

"Yes, and once we realized what it could do, how intrusive it was, we needed that vial back before you understood what we'd done."

Maggie shook her head. "So the tire—"

"Was to slow you down so Scott could get to your apartment and retrieve the vial. We'd tried your office but it wasn't there."

"We didn't mean to scare you," Scott broke in, with apology in his voice. "But we knew we had to destroy it, before it got into the wrong hands. Now that you know what it is, you can understand that, can't you?"

"What hands could it have fallen into?" she asked. "I didn't even know what I had."

"No, but others did. Alice, for instance. She was here working late the night we discovered what we'd done."

"Alice is just an intern. She wouldn't—"

"Don't be naïve," Tim snapped. "This stuff is worth millions. People have died for far less."

At that, Jacob shifted closer to Maggie and reached for her hand. "No one's dying."

"Oh, no, don't worry." Scott lifted his hands. "We don't want to hurt you, either of you. We just want the lotion back, Maggie, that's all."

Slipping her hand into her pocket, where she had the vial, she shook her head. "I used the last of it this morning, it's all gone."

"You're lying." Tim didn't look quite as congenial as his brother. "Okay, here's what you're going to do. You're going to hand it over."

"No, *here's* what we're going to do," Jacob said evenly. "We're going to leave. Come on, Maggie." He pulled her with him around the desk, heading toward the door, but two things happened simultaneously. Tim stepped in front of the door, which opened, hard enough to knock him to his knees.

And then Alice entered. She lifted a gun and pointed it directly at Maggie.

Chapter 10

"New plan," Alice said, with a sweet smile, the gun on Maggie, whose heart had all but stopped. "*I* get the lotion. Any objections? None? Good."

"Alice, what the hell is this?" Scott demanded.

"Oh, I forgot to mention. See, I need the lotion to catch my lying, cheating, soon to be ex-boyfriend in the act. Hand it over."

No one moved, and Alice shook her head. "Okay, listen up, people! I'm PMSing and hormonal, and when my grandma discovers I've borrowed her heat, she's going to go postal. So hand over the lotion pronto or I start taking out kneecaps, Soprano-style."

Tim pointed at Maggie. "She's got the vial."

Maggie gasped. "I do not."

"Yes," Scott said. "You do. We know you do because you clearly used the lotion and now you're trackable. You're on that screen right there, sending us your signals, see?" To show Alice, he twisted the computer screen around, pointing to the heart monitor. "This is Maggie."

Alice squinted at the screen. "How do I know?"

"Look at the history." Tim leaned over his brother and clicked a few keys on the keyboard. "See, look. She's all work and no play during the day. Now look at her nights—quiet, every single one. Typical boring scientist life—"

"Hey," Maggie said.

"Sorry, but it's true—" Tim broke off with a frown. "Wait a minute."

"What?" Alice demanded, staring at whatever they were looking at. "What's that?"

"She had sex." His fingers sped over the keyboard. "Here in this building." His head whipped around so he could look at her. "Jesus, *you had sex here?*"

Maggie did her best not to look at Jacob. "You want to discuss my sex life, now? With a gun on us?"

"Alice," Tim demanded. "Put the gun down."

"Not until I get that lotion!" Alice was looking quite unstable. She gestured the gun toward Maggie. "Hand it over."

Oh, God. If she handed over the lotion, someone might be able to eventually reproduce it, and that couldn't be allowed to happen. "Did you know Mary Stuart became the Queen of Scotland when she was only six days old?"

Alice cocked her gun. "Maggie, I swear to God, those quirky little facts were cute, oh . . . never. Okay? So please, shut up and *give me the lotion.*"

"Honey," Jacob said, squeezing Maggie's fingers, giving her a long look. "Give her what she wants. Give her the lotion."

Maggie stared at him. *Honey?*

"The jig is up," he said quietly. "So just give her the lotion. *Honey.*"

Honey. Of course! The honey lotion in her lab, the one he'd slathered on her and lapped off her breasts. "Right," she said, trying not to be disappointed that he wasn't calling her honey. "You're right. I'll go get it, but you're coming with me."

"Fine," Alice said, through her teeth. "But do it fast. While you're gone, Scott's going to make me a copy of the software required to go with the stuff." She waved at the windows. "Because I'm going directly to the asshole's apartment, putting the lotion on him, and catching him in the act of fucking his lab partner, and I'm doing that today, so hurry the hell up."

"Go," Tim said to Maggie and Jacob. "Quickly."

"And remember I can see your heart rate on the screen *and* your location, so no running away. And no more sex. No one gets any more sex until *I* get sex!"

"Maybe we should add Midol to the lotion," Jacob murmured into Maggie's ear, as they ran into her office, where she grabbed her honey potion. Turning back, she saw Jacob hitting 9-1-1 on his cell.

"She's got a gun—"

"Just get the honey lotion in a vial."

She did just that, her gaze on Jacob speaking quietly and quickly to emergency dispatch, looking so big and tough and . . . hers, dammit. If something happened to him she'd never forgive herself. She put a stopper in the new vial. "Okay, let's do this. But once she leaves with this vial, you're out of here. It won't fool her for long."

"We're *both* out of here."

"Deal." Her voice cracked a little, and she dropped her gaze, staring at his chest. "I couldn't handle it if anything happened to you, Jacob. I really couldn't. Listen, I know I totally took advantage of you with that whole Mr. Wrong thing—"

"Whoa. There were *two* of us making that decision. I wanted you, too."

"We're different."

Irritation flashed across his face. "We've discussed this, Maggie."

"You know what I mean."

"Did you know if you had enough water to fill one million goldfish bowls, you could fill an entire stadium?" he asked.

She blinked. "Um, what?"

"Yeah. And if you flew from London to New York by *Concorde,* due to the time zones crossed, you would arrive two hours before you left."

She let out a low laugh. "What are you doing? Did you look those up for me?"

He held up his hand. "One more. I don't want this to be a one-time thing."

Her amusement vanished as fast as it'd come. She swallowed hard but the sudden lump of emotion wouldn't go down. "Jacob."

"It's so much more for me. It's always been more. I'm not sure exactly when it happened, whether it was the way you look at work when you're concentrating, with your wild hair and fascinating brain, or how you make me smile all the time, or maybe it's that you always have a pen behind your ear—"

"What? I don't—"

Reaching over, he pulled a pen out from behind her ear.

"And your neck?" he whispered. "*Always* smells amazing. And then there's the way you look first thing in the morning, when you open your eyes and see me."

She let out a surprised laugh. "That was once."

"Yeah, but we can fix that. And then there's your laugh, that goofy, self-conscious laugh. It melts my damn heart every time. So you should know, it's not just a one-time thing, not anywhere close. I'm in love with you, Maggie."

Before she could respond, Alice screamed through the walls. "Why is your heart rate going up? Goddammit, are you getting naked?"

Maggie couldn't hear anything past the roar of her own blood in her ears, and those three words still echoing between her ears.

He loved her.

Loved her . . . "Jacob—"

"Maggie!" Tim yelled. "She's going to start shooting. Get back in here!"

"Come on." Jacob led her back into Scott's office, and Maggie, her heart still racing over what Jacob had just said, handed the vial over to Alice.

"Wait." Tim was staring at the vial.

Maggie froze. Obviously, the color was off, and he knew it. She locked gazes with him, holding her breath.

"You had a lot left," he finally said.

"Yeah. I did." *Crap.* Maggie turned to Alice. "You know how illegal this is, right?"

"Yes, because waving a gun in your face isn't illegal at all." Alice jammed the vial into her pocket and pulled out a fistful of cuff ties from her other. "Look, I'm sorry, all right?" She cuffed Scott to his filing cabinet and Tim to the desk. Then she came up to Maggie and Jacob, and after a hesitation, hooked them together. "For you," she whispered to Maggie. "Because he looks to be a keeper, someone you'd never need this lotion for."

Jacob didn't say a word but there was a muscle ticking in his jaw.

"Don't do this, Alice," Maggie begged her. "It's not too late to—" She broke off when Jacob jerked his arm—and therefore hers as well—hitting the button on Tim's desk that activated the magnetic couch.

The couch shot straight up from the floor, coming to a hover about two feet above the carpet, causing a handful of objects to instantaneously fly through the air as if hurled by a slingshot—like Scott's phone, which nearly hit Tim, and . . . the gun, which was yanked right out of Alice's hands.

It slapped hard to the couch and stuck there.

"Dammit!" Alice yelled as Tim used his leg to trip her to the floor. Still attached to the filing cabinet, he slid down and sat on her.

"Hey!" she yelled, struggling. "I'll sue you for sexual harassment!"

"I'm gay," Tim informed her dryly. "I'm more likely to sexually harass Maggie's hottie than you, trust me."

Maggie stared at her "hottie"—the one who loved her—her free hand clutching her heart, because it had only just now started beating again. "Did you mean it?"

Jacob's eyes softened, and some of the tenseness left his body as he lifted his free hand and cupped her face. "Yes, I meant it."

"Oh, God. I love you, too." Her throat was so tight she could hardly speak. "For so many reasons. You say what you think and you do what you say, and you've got more logic and common sense in your pinkie than my last five dates combined."

"Hey," Scott said, insulted.

Maggie ignored him. "I think you're the smartest, funniest, sharpest, man I've ever met."

"I could have said what I thought and what I feel," Scott muttered to Tim. "I could be solid and loyal."

Jacob pulled Maggie close. On Scott's desk, her heart monitor was still going nuts. With her free hand, she pulled the vial Tim had given her out of her pocket and smashed it to the floor. "That was the last of it," she told her soon-to-be ex-bosses. "I realize you can make more, but if you do, know this—I'll turn Data Tech over to the FDA, the DFA, the CIA, and the DEA, and whoever else will listen to me."

"You're bluffing," Tim said. "Your work is your life. And without us, you won't get funding."

"I'll wait for the right funding, I'll find it eventually."

"It could take years."

"Maybe." She looked at Jacob. "But I'll wait. My life is no longer just my work."

His eyes were full of affection and heat, lots of heat. "I like the way you think," he said, as pounding footsteps came down the hallway just outside the door.

Knowing it had to be the police, Maggie linked her fingers with Jacob's. "This is going to get messy, and might take some time to sort out. After which, I'm going to be unemployed." She winced. "Merry Christmas to me."

"I love messy. And I love you. As for the unemployed at Christmas, don't worry, I have an in with Santa. Have you been naughty or nice?"

"Nice."

"Well, we'll have to work on that," he murmured, just as the police burst through the door.

It took several hours to sort everything out, but eventually, Alice ended up in jail, Tim and Scott lawyered up, and Maggie and Jacob were free to go. Maggie walked out of the room where she'd been questioned and found Jacob waiting for her.

He looked into her face and slowly held up a little bough of mistletoe over his head.

She couldn't help but smile when she looked at him. "What's that?"

"A hint of what I want from you."

"And after the kiss?"

"More."

"More?"

"I want it all, Maggie. And I'm hoping you do, too."

"Yes." And she walked right into his waiting arms.

Bah, Handsome!

Chapter 1

Outside the weather was as the song went—frightful. Inside, Hope O'Brien looked down at the huge box of Christmas decorations she'd dug out of the cellar of her bed-and-breakfast inn and thought maybe *this* would be the year that Santa brought her something she needed. Money to meet her bills for the month would be nice, or lacking that, maybe an orgasm.

Yeah, now that would be *real* nice.

Smiling at the thought, she pulled out some brightly colored balls and ribbons and—

"Mistletoe!" Lori snatched up the dried sprig, and held it to her chest like it was a bar of gold.

Hope slid her best friend a look as wind continued to batter the small B&B around them. "You've been married six months and still drag Ben into the closet whenever you see him. What could you possibly need with mistletoe?"

Lori, also the support staff for the inn, waggled a brow. "It's for you."

"You want to kiss me? Well, why didn't you just say so?" Hope leaned in and puckered up. "Give me your best shot."

Laughing, Lori shoved her away. *"I* don't want to kiss you. I want someone *else* to kiss you. A penis-carrying someone."

"Yeah." Hope sighed. "I think that ship's sailed."

"Honey, you're twenty-nine. That ship has not sailed. You're just being a pansy-ass because your last boyfriend stole all your money and ruined your credit before going to jail, forcing you to go begging from your asshole-rich stepbrother."

"Gee, thanks for the recap."

"And you're probably also still feeling the effects from your boyfriend before that, the one who stole your self-confidence. What was his name? *Dickwad?"*

"Derek," she murmured. *Derek the Dickwad.* "And you wonder why I say my ship has sailed. Clearly I can't trust my own judgment."

Lori's eyes softened, and she leaned over to squeeze Hope's hand. "That's because you don't trust your heart. Look, you're pragmatic and tough—you've had to be. But let's face facts. You have a type, and that's the badasses. Joey, Dickwad . . ."

True. Hope had always been a sucker for the bad boy. Someone had once told her it was from growing up without a father figure, but she didn't believe in letting circumstance mold her. She was a "be responsible for your own destiny" sort of woman.

Lori twirled the mistletoe in her fingers. "Did you know if you wish on this stuff, it'll come true."

"Yes, and maybe Santa's reindeers will sprinkle magic dust over all the land and make us rich."

Lori gave her the puppy dog eyes. "Are you really going to suck all the spirit out of the holiday?"

Hope rolled her eyes, but then shook her head. "No."

"Then *wish*, dammit."

"Fine." Hope snatched the mistletoe and closed her eyes. "I wish that the DA would shake my money out of Joey so I can pay back my brother before he calls the loan that's due on January first, which is in . . ." She mentally calculated. *Oh, God.* "Twenty-one days."

"Oh, Hope," Lori said sadly, making Hope realize she was doing it, she *was* sucking the spirit out of the holiday.

"Okay, you're right. Let's try this." Hope paused, the only sound being the vicious storm currently rattling the windows. "I wish for someone to hang up all the Christmas decorations for me. And . . . clear them up after Christmas."

Lori's eyes were censoring. "Stop thinking of the B&B first; think of you. *You*, Hope. Wish for . . . *sex*. Yeah, now *there's* something you could use. How long has it been anyway, six months?"

Six months sounded pathetic, but the truth was even more so. She lifted a shoulder.

"*Eight* months?"

Fourteen, but who was counting? Oh, wait. She was. She was counting.

"Give me that." Lori grabbed the sprig back, once again pressing it to her heart and closing her eyes. In sweet earnest, she said, "Hope's too busy and stressed to think of herself so I'm doing it for her. I wish for a penis for her. One that's attached to a man who knows how to use it."

"It's no use." Hope shook her head even as she laughed. "I'm done with badasses, penises and all."

"A really *good* man," Lori went on, eyes still closed. "Not a badass, but a kind, gentle soul—but good in bed. I can't stress that enough."

"That's funny."

Lori opened her eyes and reached into her pocket, from which she pulled out a string of four condoms. "Merry early Christmas."

"You are not serious."

Lori merely stuffed them into Hope's jean pocket.

Hope laughed again, then raised a brow when someone knocked on the front door of the B&B. Though it was only six in the evening, it was pitch-black, with the snowstorm still raging out there. "Huh."

"Maybe it's him," Lori whispered.

"Him who?"

"The man I just wished for you, the one with the kind, gentle soul. And the penis he knows how to use."

Hope rose from the dining room table where they'd been sitting. She supposed it could be an unexpected guest. She had six guest rooms, and only two were filled at the moment; her guests either in their rooms or in front of the fire she had roaring in the living room. She'd be happier with more paying guests, but what with the B&B being out in the boondocks two hours north of Denver, and the economy in the toilet, things were slow.

Of course now was the worst possible time for her to be slow, what with her bank accounts emptied and all. She was hanging on by a thread—a thread that had come from her stepbrother Edward, a guy who made Scrooge look like Santa Claus.

It was killing her, knowing she'd been forced to borrow from him, but it was also temporary.

As in a lump payment was due to him in LA by January 1 . . . Twenty-one days . . .

She'd e-mailed Edward—he didn't do personal contact—to ask for a little teeny tiny extension, but she hadn't heard back yet.

Don't go there now, she told herself, and moved toward the foyer, followed by Lori. She opened the front door and was immediately assaulted by the wind and snow. She squinted past it to take in the tall, dark stranger who was dressed as if he'd just walked off the cover of a glossy man's magazine.

"Does it always snow like this?" he asked, stomping the

snow from his boots, his voice low and husky as if he was half frozen.

Tall, dark and *irritated,* she corrected. "In December, yes. Can I help you?"

He squinted through his glasses past snowflakes the size of dinner plates. "My car got stuck about a half mile back."

Behind her, Lori gave her a little nudge. *See? There he is, the penis I wished for.*

Hope ignored her as she eyed the guy on her step. He had his hood up. Sure his voice sounded fine, even attractive, but that didn't make him a good guy. Until she saw his face, she wasn't letting her guard down. "Four-wheel drive?" she asked him.

"No, it's a rental. I have chains on it, though."

So he wasn't a local. "Yeah, not good enough, not on a night like this one." His clothes screamed big city, from his fancy coat down to his fancy boots. Maybe New York, maybe Los Angeles—either way he was definitely *not* used to Colorado winter driving. "If you'd like to rent a room for the night, I can get you help digging out your car in the morning."

"Yeah, okay. Thanks."

When she moved back and opened the door wider, he stepped inside, giving her a brief impression of a lanky lean build, but not much else. He smelled good, though. Woodsy, citrusy . . . masculine.

He turned to her then and let his hood fall back as he opened his coat, looking at her with a hint of wariness as if he was waiting for something, which came immediately.

Recognition.

As it hit her, she went still. Danny Shaw, her stepbrother's CPA. He had a striking face, she'd give him that. High cheekbones, rich mahogany eyes slightly magnified by the sophisticated wire-rimmed glasses on his nose. His hair matched his eyes and was trimmed short. With his coat open, she could see his tailored pants and shirt, both undoubtedly as expensive as his glasses. If she hadn't known him, she'd have taken another minute to fully appreciate his fine form.

But she did know him, and all the friendly drained from her, replaced by tension. "Did you come to give me an extension?"

"Unfortunately, no."

She felt the air leave her lungs as if he'd hit her. "Then get out."

"We need to talk, Hope."

"No." She hauled open the door again, ignoring the snow that pelted her. *"Get out."*

"Hope," Lori murmured. "Who is this, another ex-boyfriend?"

"No. Worse. Meet Danny Shaw, my brother's lackey. And I still have three weeks left." She jerked her head toward outside. "Good-bye, Danny."

"You just offered me a room." His voice was very distinctive with its low, husky timber, and she kicked herself for not recognizing it sooner. After all, she'd met with him when negotiating the loan from Edward, because heaven forbid Edward get his hands dirty with the details.

And the details *had* been dirty. Edward hadn't exactly given her a favorable loan. Nope, he'd been less than one step from a loan shark, but she'd figured go with the devil she knew . . . "I've just unoffered the room," she said, once again gesturing for him to go. "You're letting out all my bought air."

"We really need to talk first, Hope."

"Sorry, but I don't talk to rat bastards."

He raised a brow. "Rat bastard is what you call your brother."

"Yes, and as Edward's representative, you get the same consideration. Get out, Danny. Go home. Tell him I'll get him his money on time." Since he didn't budge, she grabbed his hand and pulled him to the door. He stepped over the threshold, then turned back to face her to say something.

But she shut the door in his face.

*   *   *

Danny let out a shuddery breath. Shuddery because he was a minute away from freezing his nuts off. When he'd flown out of Los Angeles that morning, it'd been sunny and a slightly chilly sixty-eight degrees.

Ha. He hadn't known chilly. He hadn't known a lot of things, such as how bad the rental car would be, or the depths of Hope's worry and fear. He wrapped his coat tighter around him and pulled his hood back up before once again knocking on the door.

She didn't answer, but he would have sworn he could hear her breathing through the wood. Hope, of the pretty strawberry blond hair that was slipping out of its ponytail and into her eyes, which were so blue he could have drowned in them. Hope, of the petite, willowy frame that hid an inner strength of steel. That strength shouldn't have surprised him; after all she was an O'Brien. "Come on, Hope. Let me in."

More of her loaded nothing, and he sighed, shoving his hands in his pockets and hunching his shoulders against the wind as if that would help. Christ, why would anyone choose to live here? "Look, I should have called first, okay? But if I had, you wouldn't have agreed to see me."

As proven by the loaded silence.

"I realize you'd like me to just leave," he said. And he'd love to do that. Hell, he missed LA already. He was wet and cold and hungry, and as far as he could tell there was no food in his immediate future. No four-star hotels, either. Nothing but wide open spaces and the utter lack of civilization.

He was on a whole other planet. "I'll freeze to death out here, Hope, you know that. You don't want my death on your hands, do you?" Okay, stupid question. She'd welcome his death and stomp on his grave.

He'd met her for the first time two years ago when she was leaving Los Angeles. She'd come to Edward's office to say good-bye, but Edward had been in a meeting and hadn't bothered to come out—the guy wasn't big on family.

The last time Danny had seen Hope was three months ago when she'd needed money. Once again, it'd been Danny to deal with her, and he'd laid out the terms that Eddie had insisted on—the terms *not* in her favor.

Danny had looked into Hope's eyes as he'd done Edward's dirty work and felt like a complete jerk offering her such a crappy deal. Knowing he could lose his job, he'd shut the file, gone against his duties, and advised her not to sign.

But she'd signed anyway.

"Letting me die out here will only make things worse," he said now. "Come on, Hope. Open up."

"Just leave."

He wished he could. But he had a job to do and that was to protect Edward's investment. Didn't matter that Edward was a miserly ass who got his jollies over lording it over people, one of those people being his own sister. What mattered, unfortunately for Hope, was that Edward now held the loan on both the land and the B&B itself, and after her extension request, now wanted the situation assessed.

Which is where Danny came in.

Not the most comfortable situation, given that his rental car was truly stuck. Turning away from the front door, he stared out into the nasty storm knowing he had two choices: beg some more, or strike out on foot back to his car where he could run the motor for heat until he ran out of gas. Neither option appealed, but he had a feeling that no amount of begging would work, so he stepped off the top step and into the snow.

Shit, it was cold.

Behind him the door whipped open. "Are you crazy?" Hope demanded to know. "You really will freeze to death if you walk back to your car."

"So you're going to let me in?"

She seemed to gnash on her teeth over that one. She was wearing snug hip-hugging jeans that were frayed at the waist and hem, and torn over one knee. Her long-sleeved v-necked tee revealed sweet curves, and proof that she was chilled. "It's going to cost you," she finally said.

Yeah, he was getting that. "I'm willing to pay your rate."

"For rat bastards, it's double."

He looked into her stubborn, beautiful face and saw that she meant it. "Fine. Double."

"Did I say double? I meant triple."

Her eyes were intense, protective, and dammit.

Hurt.

And wasn't that just the crux. Edward was such an ass. So determined to rise from the gutter from which he'd been born, he was perfectly willing to walk over his own family. Even worse was the knowledge that Hope was trying to do the same, trying to change her life and circumstances, and was getting a bad deal.

But she wasn't his job. God-damn, he really hated when his morals bumped up against the source of his income. "Just name the price, Hope."

She shoved her long bangs off her face and thought about it.

How any woman could look so sweet and soft, and yet be so fierce, was beyond him, but somehow she pulled it off.

"You might want to consider that I'm standing here with my wallet open and you need the money," he pointed out.

Okay, not his smartest move, reminding her that she was in trouble; he knew it even before her eyes chilled and her mouth tightened.

She had a pretty mouth.

Not that he was noticing. "Look," he said quickly. "The roads are bad, there's no other hotel nearby, and I'm stuck. Whatever you want."

"I want a better-termed loan."

"Except that."

She looked at him, proud and desperate, and he felt a crack in his armor.

Not good.

"I'd do it if I could," he said quietly.

"Would you?"

"In a heartbeat." He shifted and lowered his voice. "I asked you not to sign—"

"Don't." She pushed him back a step and pointed at him. "Don't. I'm well aware that *I* screwed this up, and no one else." A sigh escaped her, and once again, she shoved her hair back. "You can have a damn room."

"Thank you."

"Just get inside." She shut the door, behind him this time, still looking deceptively soft and sweet. "You're shivering like a pansy-assed little girl."

Chapter 2

Hope easily kept busy for the next hour, meaning she paid no attention whatsoever to her unwelcome houseguest.

Or pretended to pay no attention . . .

The only meal she served at the B&B was breakfast, but she did offer drinks in the evenings. Tonight they served eggnog to go with the festive decorations she was still working on, and in the living room people intermingled, having a good time.

Hope was making sure of it.

She considered that a part of her job, and she enjoyed it. She enjoyed the camaraderie, the easy alliances of perfect strangers brought together for short periods of time. She enjoyed hearing people's stories and tonight should have been no exception.

Except she was so painfully, acutely aware of the tall, lanky man leaning against the mantel. She eyed him critically, prepared to toss him out on his bony ass if he tried to stir up trouble, but he didn't. He stood there in his sophisticated clothes and those wire-rimmed glasses, looking as if he could walk into a boardroom, or an elegant dinner.

Or a casual B&B with a bunch of strangers.

He smiled easily, talked just as easily, effortlessly infusing himself into the conversation with her guests as if he belonged. When asked, he said he was there on business but hoped to take some time for fun, freely admitting he wasn't much of an outdoors person but that he was open to new experiences.

She wondered what new experiences exactly he referred to, and how it sounded vaguely sexual to her, even as she wondered how he'd like the experience of her foot up his ass if he so much as hinted that he was here because she'd screwed up financially.

But he didn't.

After the guests went up to their rooms, she was in the kitchen cleaning up when Danny came in carrying dirty glasses, setting them into the sink.

"Guests don't do the dishes," she informed him.

He merely shoved up his sleeves and dug in. "We both know I'm not a real guest." He turned his head to look at her. *Really* look at her. As if maybe he could see in past the brick wall she'd so carefully built around her emotions and private feelings over the years.

That was new.

And not in any way welcome.

"I pull my weight," he said. "Always."

Now *that* she understood, and she put a hand over his in the sink, surprised to find his warm—she'd imagined they'd be as cold as his heart. Except she was beginning to doubt that was true. "You didn't have to come, you know. I'll get the money."

One way or another . . .

He was close. Close enough that she could have bumped his body with hers as she tipped her head up and looked past his lenses and into his eyes, which weren't just a solid light brown, but had gold swirling in the mix and were as surprisingly warm as his hands.

"I'm glad to hear it," he said.

"Are you?"

There was a beat of silence, and in it, much of the good-natured humor drained from him, which she found oddly unsettling. He was more sincere than she'd given him credit for.

And tougher.

And something else, too, something that surprised her. He was kind of sexy with that intense, intellectual gaze behind those glasses.

"You think I want you to fail," he finally said with a hint of disbelief.

"I think that would suit Edward, taking this place from me even though he could care less about it. He could probably sell the property in a blink, and, poof, make condos appear, or something else with lots of concrete."

Danny opened his mouth, then slowly shut it again. Hard to argue the truth, apparently. After a moment he shook his head and flashed her a rather grim smile, full of no amusement at all and maybe even some hurt. "The fact is, Hope, I'm here only because your brother wants to make sure the terms of the loan are going to be met, nothing personal. It's just the job. It's business," he said with soft steel. "That's it."

"The terms will be met," she said with equal soft steel. "So you can go home and report just that."

"As I'm snowed in, we appear to be stuck with each other for now. And since we are, maybe I can help. If you showed me your financials—"

"No." She shook her head. "Nothing personal," she said, sending his own words back at him. "But I don't need your help."

He looked at her, and she'd have sworn she saw a brief flash of empathy, even respect. And also frustration with some caring mixed in.

Which was impossible, she told herself, since he was a rat bastard, and rat bastards didn't care.

* * *

As always, Hope woke up at the crack of dawn. It was a life-long habit. When she was little, her father died from a heart attack, and she'd get up early to make toast and tea for her stricken mother.

Later, after her mother remarried and divorced two more times, Hope still got up early to work at a resort, where she'd cook from dawn until the start of high school since Edward had gone off to college without looking back. Mother had never really recovered from her losses.

Hope had always kept up the early-morning habit because she liked getting things done during those hours when everyone else was snoozing away, but this morning, she suddenly wished she'd developed a different habit.

Like flying south for the winter.

Because this morning, lying in bed in the dark dawn, she kept thinking about the unwelcome guest she had upstairs.

Danny Shaw. He was Clark Kent on the outside and sheer, determined Superman steel on the inside.

And he didn't think she could do this.

Facing that fact made her feel better. Because facing it, she could fight it, do something about it.

Kicking off her covers, she got out of bed and shivered. Holy smokes, it was a cold one. The thermometer on her window said five.

As in five degrees.

And it was still snowing like a mother. She needed to stack some more wood today. She also needed to clear snow and put up the rest of the decorations.

But it wasn't until she stood in her bathroom that she realized her biggest problem. She had her toothbrush in one hand and a mouthful of toothpaste as she stared into the bathroom sink; the handle cranked to full blast, no water coming through.

The pipes were frozen.

"Oh no, no, no, no . . ." Not today, not when she needed to make a *great* impression. Not when she needed Danny to think everything was perfect.

Dammit.

Obviously, the place wasn't perfect. It was built in the 1940s by a wealthy mine owner as a vacation home, then renovated in the '80s by the family of the original owner. Currently the place was in some fairly desperate need of more updates and renovations, which she was getting to on an as-needed basis.

Like the plumbing problems.

And unfortunately, there were other problems as well. Upstairs were the guest bedrooms, which needed paint. Downstairs were the kitchen, dining room, living room, and social area, and a small but quaint servants' quarters off the kitchen where Hope lived.

All of which also needed paint.

And more.

Lori and her new husband Ben, a local handyman, lived about a mile down the road in their own place. Hope could call Ben about the pipes. He'd snowmobile here in a heartbeat, but if she'd learned anything in her twenty-nine and three-quarters years of life, it was to do for herself whenever possible.

Even when it seemed impossible.

The bottom line was that the B&B was everything to her. She'd certainly put everything she had in it, and not just money, but her heart and soul. It was the first thing that had been entirely hers, and having people come and stay and enjoy the Colorado mountains—the hiking, biking, skiing, or whatever they'd come to the wilderness for—never failed to thrill.

It was a world away from where she'd grown up in Los Angeles, in the heart of the city, and a world away from the rat race that had once threatened to consume her when she'd lived and worked there as a chef. Now, here, in the silent magnitude of the magnificent Rocky Mountains, she'd found tranquility and peace.

And frozen pipes. She spit out her toothpaste and looked down at her thin, loose cotton pj bottoms and cami. She added on a pair of thick sweats, a scarf, a knit hat, her down jacket, and her imitation Ugg boots.

She caught sight of herself in the mirror—the Pillsbury Dough Woman—and laughed. Good thing she didn't have a man in her life, she thought as she grabbed her blow-dryer and headed into the kitchen, where she added an extension cord to her arsenal. She plugged the cord into an outlet on the counter, then carefully propped open the cellar door with a large can of beans because it had a tendency to shut and lock.

The stairs made a heck of a racket, which oddly enough had always comforted her. She figured if the boogeyman was ever going to climb the stairs to get to her, she'd at least hear him coming.

In the cellar, she eyed the pipes, indeed frozen solid. "Please work," she said, and stretched out on the ground underneath the pipes and turned the blow-dryer on high.

Two minutes later the pipes were still frozen solid, but *she* was warming up nicely, and she blew her out-of-control bangs out of her face to see better. If she'd had a pair of scissors with her, she'd have cut them off right then and there.

She heard someone come down the stairs, and then a set of shoes appeared at her shoulder.

Nikes, brand-new. Size—at least twelve.

"Your pipes are frozen," the Nikes said.

She didn't look up. Maybe if she didn't, Mr. Big City Know It All Rat Bastard would go away. Far away. "I'm on it." She readjusted the heat coming from the blow-dryer and concentrated, picturing the pipes melting because, hey, you had to dream it to live it—

Danny crouched at her side, his legs at least a damn mile long. She'd always thought of him as a little on the skinny side, but with his pants stretched taut against him, she could see that those legs actually had quite the definition of muscle to them. She glanced up the length of them.

And up.

Yep, those pants were expensive. Probably worth more than all the clothes in her closet. Which, as she tended to live in jeans and tees, wasn't saying that much.

"Need any help?" he asked.

"I can handle it." She made the mistake of turning her head and meeting his gaze. First of all, it was barely the crack of dawn and yet there he was, dressed as if he was going into the office, with a button-down shirt and pullover sweater in a deep royal blue that seemed so soft and yummy she almost forgot he was not only Nerd Central but also capable of siccing Edward on her.

And he smelled good, *again*. How that was even possible when she knew he couldn't have possibly had a hot shower, she had no idea. But he looked fresh and clean and neat, his every hair in place, his glasses revealing those warm eyes.

He'd even shaved, with what must have been an electric razor.

And she? With her multiple layers, disastrous hair and no makeup—and she was pretty sure she hadn't shaved her legs this week—she felt extremely out of place. Way to go, Hope. Way to be hot and irresistible.

Not that she cared what he thought about her appearance, but she did care very much about what he thought about how she was running this place. "Go on up," she said. "I'll handle this."

He didn't move.

She swiped her arm over her forehead. Yeah, it was getting hot in here. With one arm still holding the blow-dryer in place on the frozen pipe, she pulled off her scarf and hat, trying not to picture what her hair must look like.

His face appeared next to hers as he, without regard for those expensive clothes and the dirty floor, stretched out on his back at her side and peered at the pipe, an icon of grace and physical power.

"You're making progress," he said. "You have another blow-dryer?"

He was polished, where she was not. He was smooth and knew what to do in any social situation, where she most definitely did not. *He was her mortal enemy.*

So she had no idea why she looked at his mouth and felt an odd pang of excitement. She'd simply gone too long without a man's touch; that was what was causing this ridiculous and untimely sense of loneliness that was clearly making her lose her mind.

"Hope?"

She was still looking at his mouth. It was a really nice mouth. Probably all the better to pull his prey into his web.

He caught her staring at him and skimmed his hand up her arm. "You okay?"

Was she? His fingers were warm and sure, and his body was lying so close to hers that she could almost taste the testosterone coming off him. Tiny prickles of desire raced up her spine to the back of her neck.

Huh.

"Hope? You with me?"

"Yeah." She cleared her throat as he ran his thumb over her knuckles.

He stared down at her hand as he slowly traced her skin. "Blow-dryer?" he murmured.

Right. "Upstairs. Second bathroom beneath the sink."

She didn't have a spare blow-dryer upstairs in the second

bathroom beneath the sink, but it would get him out of her hair, because clearly his closeness was killing off her brain cells one by one.

When he left, she let out a long, careful breath. *Whew.* How in the hell she'd managed to both hate him and lust after him at the same time, she had not a single clue. . . .

Chapter 3

Alone in the cellar, Hope felt the vibration of Danny's footsteps going up the two flights of stairs. Since she was sweating, she pulled off her jacket and sweatpants and went back to blow-drying the frozen pipes. When she heard Danny coming back down, she yelled, "Don't let the cellar door shut!" just as he did exactly that.

Shit! She sat straight up and bashed her head on the now semi-frozen pipe. Stars exploded behind her eyeballs. Damn, shit, *fuck.* Rolling to her hands and knees, she crawled out from beneath the pipe, but before she could get to her feet, Danny was there on his knees, pulling her up against him.

"Are you okay?" he demanded.

"No, I'm not. You locked us in here, Genius Boy." She sucked in a breath and pressed her hands to her forehead. "And you nearly killed me."

"Didn't have to." He pulled her hands down and put his face within an inch of hers as he studied her forehead. "You almost did it on your own." He probed the spot, making her hiss in a breath. "Miraculously, you're going to live. You know your name? Mine? Where you are?"

"Hope O'Brien, Idiot, in my damn cellar."

His lips twitched. "I thought I was Genius Boy. You didn't break the skin, but you have a good-size lump. You need ice."

"Ouch," she breathed when he kept touching it.

"Aw." Lips still slightly curved, he leaned down and pressed them to her forehead.

She jerked back in shock. "What are you doing?"

"Kissing it all better." His eyes were hot silk and sweetness, one hell of an intoxicating combination, quite lethal to her resistance effort. "Did it work?"

Well, her forehead was tingling now instead of aching. And in fact, her entire body was tingling. Good Lord.

"Did it, Hope?"

Yes. "No!"

His slight smile told her he read the lie quite easily.

"We're locked in," she said through gritted teeth. "Let's worry about that."

"Are you sure?" He craned his neck to look up at the door. "Maybe—"

"Locked. In."

"Okay. So we have lots of time for you to tell me why you sent me on a wild-goose chase."

She didn't respond. Couldn't. Because he had taken her face in his hands and was staring into her eyes. "Stop that." She tried to pull back. "I'm fine. So don't even think about kissing me again." Because *she* was thinking about it enough for the two of them.

"Damn, you foiled my evil plan." But for all his joking, there was concern in his eyes and his voice, and there was something in her that reacted to that, something she didn't trust. She didn't need worry or concern, she took care of herself. Always had. "You should know, I'm only attracted to the bad boys. You don't come even close."

"I knew I should have worn my leather pants."

She heard the laugh huff out of her and shook her head at herself. Not going to be charmed by him . . . Still way too hot, she yanked off her sweatshirt and tossed it aside. She got to her feet and stalked the length of the cellar. When she whirled back, she stumbled to a halt.

Genius Boy had pulled off his sweater as well, unbuttoned a few buttons on his shirt, and shoved up his sleeves to his elbows, revealing forearms that weren't scrawny but looked surprisingly strong. "What are you doing now?"

"Your radiator kicked on. It's hot in here."

Yes. Yes, it was, and when his gaze dipped from her face to take in her pj's, the worn camisole and cotton pants that somehow she'd actually thought were a good idea, it got even hotter.

His gaze snagged on her breasts. The soft, silky material had been washed a thousand times. The pale blue was most likely a tad bit see-through. With an inward wince, she looked down at herself.

Not sheer, but thin enough to clearly see the outline of her nipples, which for some annoying reason were hard. *Bad nipples.*

"Maybe if we pound on the door and call for help . . . ?" he murmured, his voice husky and low.

She crossed her arms over her chest and shook her head. "There's no one else here."

"Lori?"

"Doesn't come on until eight."

His jaw dropped. "You're by yourself running the entire inn from evening until morning?"

She heard the disbelief, which put her back up. "It's not a big deal." She frowned. "Normally."

"It could be dangerous, Hope. You should have someone here with you at all times."

"The only danger to me is you."

"Me?" He looked horrified at the thought. "You're not afraid of me."

She didn't want to go there. "Look, my point is that I'm selective about my guests, and besides, it's not like this is the big city. Muggings are nonexistent."

"Still," he said, looking worried.

For her, she realized, and stared at him in surprise. He was worried about her.

How long had it been since someone had worried about her?

"And that plumbing should be wrapped in insulation," he pointed out. "If it was, the pipes wouldn't freeze."

"I agree. I have some renovations ahead of me."

"Do they include fixing the drain in the upstairs bathroom—which by the way, doesn't have a blow-dryer. It doesn't even have towels."

"They're in the laundry." She was well aware of the failings of this place. Ben had offered to fix the problems, but she refused to let him work ahead of what she could pay him. Things were getting done as she could afford them.

"Look," he said softly. "This place is great. It's got history and character and charm, but it needs work. You need to get better control of—"

"*Control?*" she choked out. "I realize I need some things done, and I'm getting to them, but don't you dare stand there and talk to me about control when you don't even have any over your life. You're nothing more than a lackey for a man who likes to torture the less fortunate, and—"

"Hope." He shook his head and dissolved her temper when he stepped close again. "We both know why I'm here, and that's because you're in financial trouble."

"So I've had a bad year—" She broke off when he lifted a hand to touch the bump on her forehead, which didn't hurt nearly as much as the taste of her possible failure.

His touch was so gentle that she felt thrown, as she did by his nearness. "I really thought I'd have the money back from Joey by now," she whispered.

"Have you looked into alternative financing?"

Yes. And as she was mortgaged to the teeth, she'd been laughed out of three banking institutions to date. She was working on a fourth. "Look, all I did was e-mail Edward and ask for an extension. No big deal. Instead of bothering to answer, he sent you."

"Because he doesn't give extensions," he said softly, his finger still on her.

She slapped it away. "Fine. So now I know. So just go ahead and get out of here and I'll figure something else out."

"Door's locked," he pointed out calmly. "But after we get out, I'll—"

"Damn-A-straight you'll go."

"—help you, however you need," he said with infuriating patience.

"I already told you, I don't need your help."

"Maybe I could—"

"I said no."

He merely looked at her in that quiet and steady way he had, except . . .

Except not. They were toe-to-toe, standing just a little too close, and suddenly she realized she was breathing just a little too hard. But so was he.

Why did he have to be so . . . sexy? Because that really wasn't a fair distribution of the goods. And what the hell was he thinking about when he looked at her like that, with his eyes so heated behind those glasses? She didn't know, but he leaned in a little, and she did the same, letting out a soft, anticipatory breath as—

At the top of the stairs, the door opened. Lori stuck her head in and peered down at them. "Hey, did you guys know you were locked in?"

Chapter 4

Danny climbed the stairs back to his room, not thinking about his job or what he was here for or the snow, but how Hope had looked in her pj's, all hot and sweaty and so sexy he'd nearly swallowed his own tongue.

They'd bickered.

Gotten hot.

Bickered some more.

And gotten hotter. Not cold, which would have been the logical response to being locked in a cellar in the freezing alien turf he'd landed in.

But hot.

With a grim sigh, he pulled out his cell phone and called Edward.

"You get a check?" his boss asked.

That was Edward—always on a hell-bent wave to take over the planet. That had been attractive to Danny when he'd first hired on three years back, but was growing old. "Have you been out here at all? Your sister's really done something with the place."

"Did you get a check?"

Danny sighed. "She's your sister, Ed."

"Fine. Renegotiate."

"Really?" Danny asked, surprised. Relieved. "Because she's got the money coming from the lawsuit, or so she believes. A little more time would really help her out. What terms?"

"One year, triple the interest."

"What?" Danny laughed. "Come on, man. She can't afford that. No one could afford that."

"Those are the terms."

Danny's smile faded and he scrubbed a hand over his face. "You can't do this."

"Then make sure she pays on time."

"Yeah." Danny slid his phone in his pocket and shook his head. He loved handling money. Specifically, loved handling *other* people's money. Eddie's had been a challenge and a lot of fun.

But the fun had definitely gone.

Plus there was something else. He needed something more. More fun, certainly. He also needed . . . well, he wasn't sure exactly, but he was beginning to understand that he was going to have to make a change to get it.

He stripped and showered, which didn't cool him off. He'd rather still be locked in the cellar, stuck there with Hope so they could get past their differences.

And their clothes.

Yeah, and now he had that fantasy playing in his head, her naked and gorgeous and—

The thundering sound echoed around him without warning, making the entire house shudder.

Earthquake.

He grabbed a towel, threw it around his hips, and barreled out of his room, taking the stairs so fast he nearly flew, but all he could think was that those rickety old stairs in the cellar were going to collapse and trap Hope, who was still down there with Lori.

Hitting the bottom step, he pivoted toward the kitchen and crashed into Hope. The collision sent them both skidding across the tile entrance hall, and he lost his towel.

"Are you okay?" she asked.

He would be if he wasn't butt-ass naked. He grabbed his towel and resecured it, hoping she hadn't seen.

She was sitting on the floor, staring up at the ceiling in the awkward silence.

She'd seen.

"Well," she finally said. "I guess it's true what they say about a guy with big feet."

Danny felt himself blush. "That was an accident."

"Not a bad one, really. You perked the morning right up."

He closed his eyes, grateful he'd left his glasses on the counter in the bathroom so that he couldn't see worth shit.

Hope shoved her hair out of her face and let out a long breath.

"I'm sorry," he managed.

"For nearly killing me, or for flashing me?"

"There was an earthquake. Probably only a four, but I thought of the cellar stairs, and—"

"There wasn't an earthquake. It was just snow unloading off the roof and eaves."

He stared at her as she burst into laughter. "Not used to being wrong in your world, huh, Genius Boy?"

He turned his head and looked out the wall of windows of the living room, which revealed . . .

Snow.

And more snow.

It was piled high in berms along the roof line now that the roof had unloaded. *Shit.* With a sigh, he pushed to his feet, gripping his towel like it was a lifeline. He offered her a hand and she popped up so quickly that she had to put a hand out for balance, which happened to land on his chest.

A simple touch.

An accidental touch.

And yet somehow, it rocked his world. He looked into her face, braced for a mocking smile, but she appeared to be as shocked as he as she stared down at her hand on his bare skin, almost as if it were touching him against her will.

He wasn't touched a lot in his world. He had friends, some of the female persuasion, and he dated.

But it'd been a while.

So Hope's hand had a bolt of heat shooting straight through him. It weakened his knees and left a knot of anticipation in his gut.

Possibly feeling the same, but probably not, Hope shoved free of him and headed for the hallway that led to her rooms. Her pj bottoms were low on her hips, her cami not quite meeting them, revealing a strip of smooth, creamy skin low on her back. Her shoulders were bare, too, and he stood there in his towel, feeling extremely naked. "Where are you going?"

"To watch *Oprah* and eat bonbons," she said over her shoulder. "Because that's what I do, lay around all day and let this place fall apart."

"I never said that."

"I'm going to get dressed. I advise you to do the same. There's enough cracks in this old house. Oh, and I wouldn't bother with the fancy clothes." She stared back at him. "Wouldn't want you to get dirty."

The clothes he'd brought were his work clothes, but she had a point. They were good for his office, but certainly not hers. "I don't mind getting dirty."

"Hmm," was all she said, and kept moving, those thin cotton pants sagging even lower on her hips, making him wonder if she wore anything beneath. He didn't see how, which didn't help, and he gripped his towel tighter. Not that it mattered, she'd seen everything he had to see.

Plus she was already gone.

The storm had dumped four feet of fresh snow overnight, rendering Danny's car completely useless and also temporarily closing the roads.

Since Hope had made it clear what she thought of him being around, he decided to get some work done while she cooked up a breakfast for her guests. Problem was, the Internet connection was shoddy. The only place to get a steady connection was at the kitchen table, which apparently put him in Hope's way because every time she passed by, he felt her boring holes into him with her eyes.

"The roads are closed," he told her lightly, not looking up from his laptop. "I can't leave."

"Which apparently is karma's idea of a joke." With a sigh, she moved through.

"Don't worry about her."

Danny turned to Lori, who came in the back room door taking out the trash. She was taller than Hope, darker skinned and brunette. Beautiful, and simply dressed in jeans and a hoodie sweater. "She's all bark and no bite. Well, mostly." Lori held out a mug of coffee, which he gratefully took.

And then moaned in sheer pleasure. "That's good."

"Better than Starbucks." It wasn't a question, and Lori smiled confidently when she said it. "It's Hope's homemade blend."

"She's amazing in the kitchen."

"She is. She wants her guests to go back to their life and wax poetic about their time spent here."

"You just need more of them."

"True," Lori said on a laugh. "She's working on that. Working her ass off, actually. We're having a big paint party next week—a bunch of friends are coming out, painting for her by night, skiing by day. And she's placed a bunch of strategic ads for after the first of the year, which should be just about when we get the plumbing upgrade finished." She nodded confidently. "She's going to make it, Danny."

"She's had all this time."

"Yeah, well, it's been a rough year."

"Rough how?"

"None of your business." This from Hope herself as she came into the room and gifted Lori with a frosty look.

Lori didn't back down or apologize, just smiled sweetly and handed over the second mug in her hands. "Have some caffeine, honey. You need it."

Hope rolled her eyes, but sipped the brew, then sighed in what could only be deep pleasure. Her eyes were slightly less chilly as she turned to Danny, who was still quite certain her next words would be "get out if you have to fly out." Except Lori subtly intervened, crossing directly between the two of them to walk up to a guy who'd appeared in the doorway.

"Ben," she murmured warmly, sliding her arms up around his neck and kissing him.

And kissing him.

"Ah, man. Get a room." Hope set her mug down on the counter before sighing and looking at Danny. "They're saying the roads might be cleared by four. But honestly? Probably not. Might have to stay another night."

"Let me guess. For quadruple the going rate?"

She shrugged. "Depends on how big a pain in my ass you are."

"I'll try to control myself," he said dryly. "How about we go over your books and—"

"Sorry. I have other things to do."

Lori came up for air and smiled into Hope's eyes. "It's a snow day, honey. Take a day off."

"You're the boss now?"

Ben headed directly to the refrigerator. "Lori likes to be the boss. Hey, baby, you can be the boss of me."

Lori laughed. "Already am, big guy." And she gave him another kiss.

"Oh, good God," Hope said.

Lori leaned into her husband with a silly laugh that somehow warmed Danny. Watching them banter was like watching a really great old movie. It gave him both an odd sense of comfort—they were a family, one who cared about each other—and also an even odder sense of longing.

This. This was what was missing from his life. His family lived back East and there weren't a lot of visits. His friends were nice, but they weren't a replacement for family, not like these guys clearly were.

Ben took a big bite of the bagel he'd taken from the refrigerator, squeezed his wife's ass, and sighed. "I've got to run. The gas station's electricity's on the blink." That said, he leaned in and kissed Lori again. And then, grinning, turned to Hope, who rolled her eyes but gave him a smacking kiss.

"Hey," Lori said to her. "You never kiss *me*."

"Maybe Ben kisses better than you do."

"Kiss," Lori demanded.

With another laugh—God, she was beautiful when she laughed—Hope leaned in and kissed Lori right on the grinning lips. "There. Now can we all get to work?"

Ben's mouth had fallen open. "I'll be able to work all day on that alone."

Yeah. Danny, too.

Hope took in the dazed expression on both men's faces and shook her head. "Men."

"Oh, yeah," Ben said, and headed out.

Lori grabbed her bin of cleaning supplies and followed him.

Danny walked toward Hope, who was dumping leftover breakfast dishes into the sink. "I've already proven that I can do dishes," he said. "Let me do those for you." He gave her a nudge but she didn't move out of the way. "What's the matter, you can't give up the control enough to even let me help with dishes?"

"Hey, I'm not *that* much of a control freak."

"No?"

"No." She turned to the sink and turned on the water. "Give me some room, Genius Boy. Or should I say Runs Naked Genius Boy?"

"I thought there'd been an earthquake," he repeated on a sigh as she laughed.

"Yes, and you were trying to save me."

"Yes," he said as she once again tried to nudge him away. "You could just go do something else." He reached for the dish soap.

"I could," she agreed, but didn't move.

"Maybe you want to be this close to me."

"I don't do close."

"Because you've been burned." He met her surprised gaze. "Right?"

"Right," she admitted.

"How?"

"Two exes, both assholes if you must know."

"They hurt you?"

"Not physically, no. One stole my heart, the other my money. There's nothing left of either."

"I'm sorry. About both."

"Truthfully? The money thing hurts a lot more than the heart thing."

"Which means maybe it was never really available for him to steal in the first place."

She stared at him. "Huh?"

"Maybe he didn't steal your heart at all. Maybe he just bruised it."

She thought about that as she dug into the dishes at his side, him washing, her rinsing and drying, and when she didn't say anything more, he figured that was the end of that conversation.

"Okay, you might be right," she finally said. "No one's stolen my heart, it just got run over a few times. I can't tell you how much better that makes me feel."

He laughed softly at her sarcasm. "Hey, unless you've been screwed over, you can't appreciate the good stuff. Consider it a rite of passage."

She cocked her head at him. "Have you been screwed over?"

He thought of all the girls in high school and college who'd dismissed him as a nerd. And the women since, none of whom had stuck. "I *invented* being screwed over."

She shook her head. "Are you trying to tell me you're a player, Danny?"

He laughed. "The only thing I play with any skill is Guitar Hero. All I'm saying is that we've all been hurt. Everyone has baggage. You getting ripped off by your ex is a crime, but it happens. It's how you move on with what you know now."

She arched a brow. "And what do I know now?"

"Admit your taste in men sucks."

She laughed, as he'd hoped she would. "So you're suggesting a change in men?" she asked.

"Most definitely."

"Any ideas?"

"As a matter of fact . . ."

Her laughing gaze met his. "Let me guess, I should try a nerdy brainiac who's attempting to ruin my world?"

"More like a nerdy brainiac—a very sexy one, by the way—

who's going to do his best to help you stay in control of your world."

"Funny, but I've never considered nerdy brainiacs all that sexy."

"Maybe you haven't met the right ones." He waggled a brow, stood up a little straighter, and flexed.

Which cracked her up as she slid another dish into the sink. The angle of the plate caught the stream of water and sprayed him in the chest. At first, he thought it was an accident, but then she did it again.

"Sorry," she murmured.

Sorry, his ass. He pulled the wet plate from the sink and set it on the counter. "You don't want to take me on, Hope."

"No?" She grabbed another plate, but he was quick, reaching his arms around her and bracketing her wrists with his hands.

"Okay, you're good," she admitted. "But so am I."

"Are you?" He shifted as she wriggled, pressing her between the counter and his body so that her back was plastered up against his front, her very sweet ass solid to his crotch.

At the realization, she went still.

So did he. Well every part of him except one certain part.

"Danny?"

"Yeah?" His voice sounded like his vocal cords had been roughed up with sandpaper.

The moment stretched out, humming with tension that was no longer temper or good humor, but something far more dangerous, and Hope let out a low breath. "What are we doing?"

No clue.

He turned her to face him. She looked up at him, her face quiet and solemn, but there inside the watchfulness was something else, something he'd needed to see.

Desire.

Hunger.

And her conflict over feeling those things.

Slowly he reached out for her, and just as slowly, lifted her up against him.

Her hands went to his shoulders, but she didn't push him away. Instead, she sank her fingers into him.

Letting out a breath, his mouth brushed her jaw, and he closed his eyes to better absorb the feel of her in his arms. Then she turned her head, and somehow their lips met.

At the kiss, a soft sigh escaped her, a sound of both excitement and pleasure, and he opened his mouth on hers.

God, yeah. He deepened the connection, and she met him halfway, sliding her tongue to his in a rhythm that took him from zero to full speed ahead, and only when they were both breathless and panting, did she pull away.

Eyes wide, she lifted a finger and pointed at him. But though her mouth opened, words apparently failed her. "That was . . ."

Amazing?

Perfect?

Both?

"Unexpected," she finally managed, shaking her head as if to clear it. "Clearly a fluke."

Hell if it was. "Care to test that theory?"

"No." She stepped clear when he reached for her again, and pointed at him. "You. With the amazing mouth." She gestured him away from her. "You just stay over there, since obviously, when it comes right down to it, I'm the only one with any control around here."

And with that, she left the kitchen.

Chapter 5

"Okay, here's the plan," Hope said to Lori and Ben just before noon. Ben was back from his electrical job, helping with snow removal. They all stood outside in their heavy weather gear, being dumped on by more snow as they shoveled the front walk. "We make Danny's stay miserable."

Lori stopped shoveling and leaned on her shovel, watching Ben's butt as he worked. "Why miserable?"

"Because she likes him," Ben said, still shoveling at a steady pace.

"Because he's here," Hope corrected, shooting Ben a dirty look. "Even though I've not done anything to warrant being watched over like an errant teenager."

Lori shook her head. "You're mad at your asshole brother. Which is understandable, but you can't take it out on Danny."

"Hello, he works for said asshole brother."

"If he wanted to hurt you, he'd have done so by now. Give him a chance, Hope."

"A chance for what?"

"To be the guy I wished for you."

Hope put her hands on her hips. "Are you kidding me?"

"Well, I did wish on that mistletoe, remember? I asked for a penis for you."

"I remember," she muttered in tune to Ben's laugh.

"Which should be the next logical step, given that you've already kissed him."

When Hope choked, Ben finally stopped shoveling to stare at her. "You kissed him?"

Hope looked at Lori, brow raised.

"Sorry," Lori said. "But you two were right in the middle of the kitchen. That you never even saw me tells me how good of a kisser he is." She turned to Ben with a dreamy smile. "He's a face holder."

"Easy," Ben said, and resumed shoveling.

Lori looked at Hope. "Come on, admit he's hot. In a glasses-wearing, intellectual, sexy professor sort of way."

"I could be the sexy professor," Ben said gamefully. "I'll dress up and put on some glasses." He grinned when Lori considered that with a cocked head.

"Can we *please* put aside sex for a minute?" Hope demanded. "This isn't high school."

"Hey, you're the one wanting to play high school games," Ben said. "Making his stay miserable and all."

"That's not even high school," Lori said. "That's *middle* school." She reached around behind Ben and patted his butt. "Love those jeans on you, big guy."

Ben's eyes heated. "Yeah? Or is it what's beneath the jeans?"

"Oh, my God." Hope groaned out loud. "Didn't you already knock it out today?"

"I think it's time for our midmorning quickie."

Hope drew in a sharp breath and shook her head. "You two have a serious problem." She stuck her shovel in the snow and put her hands on her hips. "I just want him gone, okay? I'm this close to making the whole thing work, all I need is some more time with no watchdogs."

"Let him help. He said he wants to." Lori tossed up her hands when Hope glared at her. "So I eavesdropped a little."

"I don't need his help. Just keep him out of my hair until the roads are clear and if you can make him miserable while you're at it," she said, only half kidding. "Just to ensure he leaves ASAP."

"Hope," Lori admonished.

"I'm kidding. Sort of. Hey, I know! Get him to help you clean. And you." She looked at Ben. "Keep him busy doing whatever you're doing today. He's a desk jockey, though, so he's probably worthless out here. Fair warning."

"I don't think so," Ben said slowly. "I think he's made of sturdier stock than you think."

"Face it, honey," Lori said. "Fate brought him. You can't mess with Fate."

"Watch me," Hope said grimly, and struck out for the house to begin *Operation: Make Danny's Stay Miserable.*

Lori watched her go, and Ben watched Lori. "I know that look," he said. "It says you have a plan. An evil plan."

"Not evil. Not exactly."

"We're on Hope's side, Lori," he said gently.

"Of course we are. Which is why we're going to help her."

"By doing as she asked."

"By doing the opposite," she corrected. "You know, the old double switcheroo."

He blinked. "Huh?"

"We're going to pretend to do as she asked, while doing the opposite."

"Let me repeat myself. Huh?"

She patted her husband on his big, beefy shoulder. "Trust me, honey. There are some wild sparks between those two."

"Yes. It's called temper."

"No, it's sexual tension. They're attracted. And more than that, he's a good guy in a shitty situation. Same with her."

"Doesn't mean they should hook up."

"She hasn't had sex in a year."

"Can't imagine going more than one day . . ."

She laughed. "I've spoiled you. Listen, all we're going to do is play Santa and give Hope a man, even if it's a temporary one."

"Lori."

"Trust me."

He laughed softly and pulled her close. "Now that's the one thing I can promise you." He pressed his jaw to hers. "For now and always."

"For now and always," she said on a sweet sigh. "That still makes my knees weak, you know that? You make my knees weak. That's all I want for Hope, Ben."

"Weak knees?"

She slid her hand up his chest and smiled. "We can pull it off. She'll thank us."

"If you say so. But if you could pull it off with your job still intact, that would be great."

After an hour of chopping wood, Hope turned and eyed the wood pile she'd made. It was shrinking instead of growing. Then she looked at the deep grooves from the wood pile to the side of the building. Someone had been doing the stacking for her without saying a word. Since that was extremely unlike Ben, and extremely unlike Lori—both of whom would do any chore needed at any time, but with their mouths working over-time—she set down her ax and leaned on the handle.

And waited.

Sure enough, within a minute, a hooded figure came from around the back of the house where the stack of wood was, brushing off his gloved hands. He was as tall as Ben, but leaner.

And wearing glasses.

She watched Danny walk toward the stack of wood without even looking at her. Back and forth he went, working with a steadiness that told her maybe he wasn't quite the desk nerd she'd convinced herself.

And since that gave her a funny little tingle in places she'd nearly forgotten she possessed, she turned to head back inside. She appreciated the help, but that didn't change the fact that he was here to assess whether she was going to be able to pay back her loan. No way around it, Danny was going to cause her trouble.

And heartache.

Because dammit, she loved this place. Loved it like it was her family, which was ridiculous. It was just a place. But it was *hers*.

The back door was locked, which was odd. Cupping her hands, she peered into the window of the kitchen. No one there. She pounded on the door, but Lori didn't appear and neither did Ben.

Which meant that they'd found themselves a closet or God knew where and were acting like bunnies again.

Terrific.

She could wade through the snow around to the other side of the building and let herself in the front door, but they hadn't cleared the snow from the side yards, and without snow shoes she'd sink up to her thighs. Not fun. Instead, she whipped out her cell phone and texted Lori.

Let me in pls.

Lori immediately texted back:

Sorry. On a supply run.

"Bullshit," Hope muttered and shoved her phone back in her pocket. No one was on a supply run, the roads were complete muck. Nope, her chef and her fix-it guy were definitely going at it.

Again.

It should have irritated the hell out of her, but instead she found herself sighing. She was happy for them, very happy, but something deep inside her wished . . . what? That she had that same thing? She'd never been one to daydream about the white wedding, white picket fence, and kid-friendly SUV.

And yet . . . She turned and leaned against the door. As far as the eye could see was nothing but a white blanket of snow and gorgeous tall pines masquerading as three-hundred-foot-tall ghosts swaying in the light breeze.

And one hardworking guy stacking wood.

Okay, so a small part of her suddenly wanted the dream, she admitted to herself as Danny dropped his last load on the stack against the house.

He took a moment to eye the job he'd just finished, then came toward her, stride determined, expression inscrutable, forcibly reminding her that the guy was capable of melting her bones.

Oh, and that he could kiss.

That thought snaked in unwelcome, and stuck. Lori had been correct, he *was* a face holder, and in possession of a very talented tongue, and—

And she wanted him. God, so much. She straightened a bit, her belly quivering in tune to her knees. His expression didn't soften as he came toward her, but it did heat. *He was going to kiss her again,* and in spite of herself, her eyes drifted shut in anticipation.

His booted feet crunched closer in the snow. A steady gait. A sure gait.

Slowing . . .

Stopping.

But the touch of his hands pulling her up to him never came. Nor did the feel of his mouth taking hers.

"See, you're not the only one who can control yourself," came his rough whisper in her ear.

Her eyes whipped open in time to catch a view of the back of him as he vanished around the corner of the building.

And it was a very nice back.

She let out a low, shaky breath. City rat bastard had a sharp wit, she'd give him that. And a good ass.

And far too much of that control she suddenly wished he didn't possess at all.

Danny thought he'd be champing at the bit to get back to LA, but there was a certain charm to the wilds of Colorado, a sort of . . . quiet calm that he liked.

Truthfully? If it wasn't for the unfairness of Hope's situation, he might have really enjoyed himself out here.

The thing was Hope was a smart woman. She'd updated all the parts of the building that she'd had to for the place to run. And according to the business plan she'd outlined for Edward, she had a clear order of what she wanted to do with the place as the money came in.

Except the money wasn't coming in.

And like most of the other problems she had, it wasn't her fault. She was paying too much on the loan to her brother. She could get a better deal, she *needed* a better deal.

He got online and downloaded her brochure. As he'd clearly

told her, she wasn't charging enough. Plain and simple. She needed to up her prices and needed to tout herself as exclusive and luxurious, both of which she had the means to be within her disposal with only a minimal amount of work on her part. She already had the first-class chef—herself—and the gorgeous setting. All she needed were those cosmetic changes: some paint, some silk sheets and down comforters to go with . . . His fingers worked the keyboard, bringing up new research on successfully run B&Bs . . .

His cell rang.

"So," Edward said without preamble. "Did she agree to the new loan?"

In that moment, Danny had never hated his job more. He really needed that change. "I was hoping you'd rethought things."

"I don't rethink."

"Yeah. Right." Danny shook his head. "Okay, you know what? That was me. *I've* rethought things. I'm not going to do this for you, Edward."

"You handle my money. Doing so is your job."

"Not anymore, it's not."

There was a sharp pause. "Are you quitting?"

Danny drew a deep breath. "Yes."

"Because of this loan?" Edward asked in disbelief.

"She's your sister."

"Step," Edward said. "*Step*sister. And I'd recall on my own mother, you know that."

It was true. Edward had never made a secret about the kind of man he was. But if Danny stayed, he'd become the same. "I'm done, Edward."

"What the hell is going on up there anyway?"

"A lot of thinking."

"Sounds like it. What are you going to do that's better than this job?"

"I'm going to start an accounting firm." A small one, for small businesses, where he could help and maybe even make a difference instead of ruin people. "Accounting and financial services."

"Come on," Edward said on a laugh. "You love big money as much as I do, you big CPA geek."

Yeah, he did. Or had. But big money meant dealing with people he didn't always like or respect, and in return, he would turn into someone he didn't like or respect, either, he felt it.

"If you walk away," Edward warned, "we're done. No crawling back when you decide you miss my millions."

"I won't miss it."

"Is this Hope's doing? Because she has that effect on people. Trust me, she drives them crazy. Just come back, and—"

"I'm snowed in. And she's not driving me crazy." Well, she was. She really, really was, but in a good way. "Good-bye, Edward."

"Hey, you tell her she still has to pay. I'll come up and get that money myself if I have to. You tell her that."

Danny hung up and looked at himself in the mirror over his dresser. Hair neat. Glasses in place. Shirt pressed and tucked in.

Jesus. He really was a fucking CPA geek.

Well, he'd just made a huge life change, he could certainly make a few more. He untucked his shirt, then laughed at himself. Wow, what a rebel. Shaking his head, he made his way downstairs. Lori had asked him to come back down, promising him a surprise in the living room, a surprise he sincerely hoped had something to do with the smell of something *delicious* baking. Stacking wood for two hours had made him as hungry as he'd ever been. Or maybe it was quitting his job.

Or maybe it was a certain stubborn, proud B&B owner who stirred him up in both a very good, and very bad, way.

He heard the banging, then turned the corner into the living room.

142 / *Jill Shalvis*

Hope stood on a six-foot ladder, wielding a staple gun and
hanging a string of Christmas lights. She wore her usual, a
long-sleeved tee and hip-hugging jeans. This time she'd added a
tool belt to the mix, which was strapped around her waist and
immediately made him hot for some reason. She had an iPod
strapped through one of her belt loops, earphones in her ears, a
Santa cap on her head.

And she was singing at the top of her considerably tone-deaf
lungs, which had him grinning. The woman could do anything,
which made her quite possibly the sexiest thing he'd ever seen.

Yeah, he'd made the right decision to quit, because there was
no way he'd ever pull out the rug from beneath her.

She deserved more.

Knowing she couldn't possibly hear him through the music
blasting in her ears, he walked into the room, getting in her line
of sight just as she executed a little ass shimmy that made him
laugh.

When she saw him, she jumped. "Sorry," he said as she
pulled out one of the earplugs. "Didn't mean to scare you."

"You didn't." Couldn't. That was the underlying message she
wordlessly imparted. "Lori's bugging me to finish decorating."

"She told me to come to the living room."

Hope's eyes narrowed as she gripped the top rung of the ladder. "She did, did she?"

"Yes."

"Well, you'll have to excuse her. She got married and her
brain turned to mush." She stretched out some more lights to
hang.

He reached up to help hold the lights for her. "Weather fore-
cast is looking pretty nasty," he noted.

"Hopefully it'll hold." She used the staple gun on the lights,
then looked down at him. "I'm sure you have other people to
gouge the soul from."

"Is that what I've done, gouge your soul?"

"No." She sighed. "I do realize you're just the messenger."

"Was. I *was* the messenger."

"What does that mean?"

"It means I quit my job."

"What?"

"Yeah. I've known for some time that I've been needing a change."

She stared at him. "You quit your job."

"I'm thinking of starting my own business, where I get to pick my clients." He was looking forward to that. "A small accounting and financial service—right up my alley." And under those circumstances, he could see himself on the *other* side. The good side. Fighting for this woman. This smart, sexy, stubborn, gorgeous woman whose only crime had been to trust a member of her family.

"Are you crazy?" she asked, backing down the ladder. "Have you seen the news? We're in a thing called a recession. Now's not a good time to be without a job."

"I'll be okay. Hope, about your loan."

"I'll be able to pay it."

"How?" he asked frankly, worried that Edward would do exactly as he'd just promised and come here himself. He slid a hand on her arm. "I saw the For Sale sign on the adjacent lot to this one, which you also own."

"Well technically, the bank owns it. But if it sells before I get my money back, then everything's good."

Except that properties weren't moving, not in this market. "What if you got investors to buy your lot?"

"Look, I realize that you no longer work for Edward, and frankly, that says a lot about you, but I'm not about to blindly trust you. I'll do this. *My* way." She reached into a bag for a fistful of greenery and looked around for a place to hang it. "Now if you'll excuse me, Lori insisted on this stuff going up." She headed for the huge, tall mantel.

"It's mistletoe."

"I think I'd know mistletoe." She stretched up to hold the stuff in place while she nailed it with the gun.

He waited until she'd reholstered the staple gun, until she'd turned to face him before putting a hand on the mantel on either side of her. Leaning in close, until their lips were only an inch apart, he waited for a reaction.

Her gaze dropped to his mouth and went to half mast.

He loved how she put herself out there, no façade, no hidden agenda. It was one of the most attractive things about her, and he shifted even closer. His mouth brushed her cheek now, then the corner of her lips, and when her hands came up to grip his shirt, he kissed her.

She immediately leaned into him, making that same soft sigh of pleasure she'd made last time, the one that made him instantly hard. She tasted like warm, sweet, giving female, like forgotten hopes and dreams, and when she moved against him and slid her tongue to his, he thought he might die of the pleasure.

"Okay," she murmured, pulling back, eyes still closed. "Maybe it's mistletoe."

He ran his thumb over a smudge of dirt on her jaw and let out a rough breath. "Yeah."

"That stuff should come with a warning." She turned, and with her tool belt slapping against her hips with every step she took, she walked out of the room.

Chapter 6

Hope strode into the kitchen and headed straight for the sink, where she downed a full glass of cold water.

It didn't help.

She stared out the window at the still falling snow and put a hand on her heart to keep it from leaping right out of her chest, because holy smokes. *Holy smokes* could that guy kiss. She set down the empty glass and found Lori standing in the doorway grinning at her.

Hope sighed. "Saw that, did you?"

"Seriously. You ever hear of behind closed doors?"

"I know. God." At least no guests had been roaming about. *Real professional, Hope.*

"Look at it this way." Lori gave her a thumbs-up. "You're doing a helluva job with that evil plan to make his visit miserable. I bet he hated that torturous tongue lashing you just gave him."

Hope thunked her head on the cabinets. "My evil plan is kaput."

"Good. Why?"

"Because he quit. He's going to start his own business, one where he doesn't have to suck the soul out of people."

"Wow. Good for him. You got to him."

Yeah. And damn if he wasn't getting to her . . .

She shoved away from the counter and headed toward her office.

"Where are you going?"

"To bury myself in paperwork." Anything to avoid reliving the past few minutes, which had been fantasy-worthy, and definitely worth reliving—neither of which she wanted to face. "And like you were helping me make him miserable. You were too busy manufacturing ways to get us together."

"I don't know what you're talking about," Lori said innocently.

"You locked me out of the house earlier. You sent him to the living room where you knew I'd be. You—"

"Wow, you've got quite the imagination."

Hope rolled her eyes. "Okay, fine. Play innocent. Just stop playing me." She hit her office, where she spent the next few hours trying to rob Paul to pay Peter, and unable to do that, did her best to handle the money situation so as to make every creditor happy.

An impossible feat.

With a sigh, she closed her eyes and tried something she hadn't tried since she'd been four and in church with her mother. She clasped her hands together and bowed her head. "God? Do you think you could do me a favor? If you help me, I promise I'll . . ." She hesitated, wracking her brain for a worthy offering. "I'll stop fantasizing about Edward's speedy death." She opened her eyes, peeked at her bank balance, and sighed in disappointment.

As usual, she was on her own.

She turned to the window, where she saw not just the snow, falling much more lightly now, but Danny, walking the perimeter of her property while simultaneously looking down at a large piece of paper in his hands.

What was he up to now?

She should just ignore him. But she could no more do that than stop thinking about how he'd kissed her. How he'd held her face and looked into her eyes before and after as if . . .

As if she meant something to him.

The thought brought a lump to her throat, which pissed her off. Pushing up from her desk, she shoved on her knit cap and grabbed her coat. Because he might have kissed her as if she was the most important thing to him at that moment, but right now he had something else on his mind.

And she wanted to know what.

And . . . and maybe, just maybe, she wanted to see if he meant something to her, too.

So she headed outside, but the cold slap of air on the porch knocked some sense into her and she hesitated.

What was she doing?

She didn't need to talk to him, she needed to ignore him. And repeating that like a mantra, she turned back to the door.

Which was locked.

"Dammit, Lori!" But the door remained locked. With a sigh, she headed toward him.

Danny walked through the snow, squinting behind his fogged-up glasses as he checked the plot map in his hands to the lot Hope had up for sale. It ran adjacent to the B&B, most of it a hill overlooking the valley far below.

A stunning view.

He knew from Hope's business plan that she wanted to build a sledding and tubing area here. She'd need equipment for the tow lift, maybe some lights to operate at night, and the sleds. Cheap—relatively speaking—and it would give her a nighttime activity for guests. Plus, she could charge for the activity and bring in additional income. He liked it, he liked all of it, and could now see the draw, see what kept her here.

The potential was amazing.

He'd always loved the city life, everything about it; the traffic, the noise, the availability of fast food ... but he could admit, there was something to this, too. Something wild and almost savage, and incredibly soothing at the same time.

Through the falling snow he caught sight of someone standing on the back porch. Jeans, a white down jacket, snow boots ... that frown.

Hope.

She was walking toward him with purposeful steps, and at the sight of her a mix of heat and wariness hit him. He couldn't remember ever feeling this way about a woman before; the intense need, mixed with a deep, abiding affection.

As he dealt with the onslaught of emotions over that, he caught yet another movement. Something small, brown ... a dog. A brown Lab, he thought, bounding up to play with him. Danny crouched low, encouraging it to come up to him—

Whoa. It wasn't a dog.

It was a *bear cub.*

He straightened and stared in shock down at the cub, now frolicking and rolling in the snow at his boots looking like the cutest thing he'd ever seen. But even he, a certified city rat, knew baby bears didn't travel alone.

And sure enough, as he looked up at Hope still coming toward them, he saw the momma bear behind her, heading for the equipment shed and trash box between him and the B&B. Even as he registered that, Hope came to a stop and slowly turned.

And came nose to nose with the momma bear. "Oh, shit."

In answer, the bear puffed itself up and let out a low but unmistakable growl.

Danny leaped forward and let out a primal yell born of sheer terror, accompanying that with waving his arms like an idiot;

that's what he'd read one was supposed to do with bears in the wild. Be big and strong and intimidating.

God, he hoped he was looking big and strong and intimidating.

He frightened the baby bear, who cried out and leaped forward to the closest tree, which it scaled in a matter of two seconds all the while whimpering for its momma—

Who turned to the new threat and looked at Danny as if maybe he was a twelve-course meal and she was suddenly starving.

Danny grabbed Hope and tugged her behind him.

Oddly enough, his life didn't flash across his eyes. Probably because Hope shoved free of him and clapped her hands loudly. At the sound, the momma bear let out a low chugging noise in her throat, along with two long lines of drool from either side of her throat as she eyed Danny. *My, but you look delicious*—

"Sorry, but he's mine," Hope told her and clapped again. With one more growl, the bear lumbered slowly off, stopping at the tree for her baby.

"Damn," Hope said. "I must give good trash. That's the fourth time this week she's been by."

Danny would have answered but he couldn't. His legs were masquerading as overcooked noodles, and he sat so abruptly on the steps of the equipment shed that his glasses half slid off.

"Danny? You okay?"

Since he wasn't at all sure, he lay back and stared up at the gorgeous sky. Snowflakes fell on him. One hit him on the nose.

"Danny?"

"Yeah."

He heard her swear softly and drop to her knees at his side, her gloved hands running over him as she tried to figure out if he was hurt.

"I'm not injured," he said. But was he okay? Maybe, if he discounted the fact that he was out in the middle of nowhere, no Thai takeout within sixty miles, actually enjoying the feel of the snow at his back soaking into his clothes. . . . And let's not forget the biggee—that he was in all likelihood falling for a woman who was right now patting him down and making him wish they weren't outside in the cold snow but somewhere warm.

And naked.

A woman he realized he wanted to fall for.

But other than that, yeah, he was just great.

Chapter 7

Adrenaline flowing, Hope leaned over Danny. She couldn't see any injuries, but the light was low and the snow falling pretty thickly.

Dammit.

Reaching behind him, she shoved open the equipment shed. "Scoot in," she demanded.

"I'm fine."

"Yeah? Well, I'm cold and wet. Scoot in."

"City girl."

Something about the roughness of his voice, with the slight—very slight—edge of humor got to her.

He got to her. "I thought you were hurt," she said as they landed on the floor of the shed.

"Told you I'm not." He pulled off his fogged glasses and cleaned them on the hem of his shirt sticking out from his jacket. "I'm tougher than you think."

Yeah. Yeah, he was. And something else she was discovering . . . she wasn't. She wasn't nearly as tough as she'd thought, or she wouldn't be so worked up right now, heart drumming, pulse racing, even as she rolled to face him. "Why did you try to get between me and that bear?"

He put on his glasses and stared at her. "I don't know, it was instinctive."

"What did you think you were going to do, save me?"

"Well . . . yeah."

Now *she* stared at *him*. "Are you crazy?"

"You can face down a bear, but I can't?"

"You don't even like me, why would you take on a damn bear for me?"

He let out a low laugh and a shake of his head. "And here I thought you were such an observant woman."

She narrowed her eyes. "What is that supposed to mean?"

"It means . . ." He reached up and touched her face, ran a finger over the small bruise she had on her forehead from when she'd managed to nearly knock herself out with the pipe in the cellar. "You're not paying attention."

"I'm paying attention." It was why her heart was pounding in her ears. "Maybe . . . maybe you're just trying to play me."

"Maybe same goes," he said evenly.

She choked on a mirthless laugh as her emotions got the best of her. Never a good thing, but she went into a flurry of motion to get as far away from him as fast as possible, except he anticipated and caught her.

She tried to twist away, but he completely negated her temper, turning into something else entirely when he pulled her down to him and pressed his mouth to hers in a long, deep, wet kiss full of such heat she nearly imploded. By the time he pulled back, she could barely speak. "I'm not a player."

"Good. Neither am I." His eyes verified that fact, and also what he felt for her. That knowledge, combined with the heat they were generating between them, nearly took her breath. But what he did next *did* take her breath. He covered her hand in his and pressed it to his chest. "I like you, Hope." His heart was drumming, steady and just a little too fast. "That's how much."

"Maybe that's adrenaline from the bear."

Eyes on her, his fingers tightened on her hand, sliding it down his chest to the zipper of his pants. Behind it, he was hard as steel. "Is that adrenaline from the bear, too?"

"Huh." Her voice wasn't too steady. "Probably not." She let her fingers play over him, loving the way that had the breath rushing from his lungs. "Some people react to adrenaline in . . . interesting ways," she said.

"No doubt. And while that bear was beautiful, my tastes in females tend toward the furless, not to mention of the human variety."

When she snorted, his hands slid beneath her coat and up her back. "Are we going to wrestle some more, Hope? Or—"

"Or," she said definitively, and fisting her hands in the front of his jacket, she covered his mouth with hers. And right there, on the hard wooden floor, with Danny on his back and the snow blowing in behind her, she straddled him.

No slouch, he slid one hand into her hair to hold her mouth to his while the other gripped her thighs, pulling her tighter against him, and when that apparently wasn't enough, he cupped her bottom and urged her to rock against him. With a helpless moan at the feel of a most impressive bulge between her legs, she had to admit—he was no lightweight. As his mouth worked its feverish way over her jaw to her ear, she pressed her face to the crook of his neck and let her eyes cross with lust. "Danny—"

"Yeah. Right." A low breath escaped her, and he let his hands fall from her to the floor at his sides. "You've come to your senses."

His pragmatic words uttered in such a desire-roughened voice only made her want him more, and she stared down into his face, into those light, warm eyes that always drew her in, and absorbed his easy acceptance of her. *Her*. For exactly who she was. "Yes," she said softly. "I've come to my senses." And still holding his gaze in hers, she pushed him farther into the shed to protect them from the show and any prying eyes, and then went for the button on his pants.

He closed his eyes and groaned when she lowered his zipper and stroked a finger down the length of him. His hips rocked up and her name tumbled from his throat in a low, rough, strangled voice.

Her knees were digging into the hard floor and she didn't care. Her own hands were rough as she shoved up his shirt to reveal a rather impressive set of abs, and with a low, muttered "thank God," his were just as rough as he wrestled with her jacket.

She tore her gloves off with her teeth because she had to touch skin to skin, then waved her arms like a bat trying to throw off the jacket—"Holy shit," she wheezed out when his icy fingers slid up her shirt.

"Sorry." But instead of stopping, he unhooked her bra and pushed it up, along with her shirt and her half-removed jacket, then with a hand spread on the small of her back, nudged her down over him.

"Danny—" His name backed up in her throat as his mouth found a breast. God. *God*. It was like the opening of a dam, as their hands fought for purchase.

"Hope—I don't have a condom."

She stared at him as reality hit, and then she remembered. "I have four!" She pulled them out of her pocket and held them up like a trophy. "The benefit of having a horny best friend who thinks I need more sex."

"God bless horny best friends," he said fervently.

Feeling the same way, she got his pants down to his thighs and he got hers open, but then they got tangled as he tried to tug the jeans off. He wrestled with the clothes for a minute, swearing when he found she also had on long underwear. "Christ, it's just like my high school dreams, where I can't get the girl naked."

"Here." Laughing, she helped kick off her pants, and then the long underwear, which caught on one of her boots. "Leave it," she gasped as his hands pulled her back over him so that once again she was straddling him, where together they got the condom on.

"God, Hope, look at you." He stroked his hand up her inner thigh, letting his thumb stroke over her very center, carefully spreading her open. "You're wet." He played in that wetness, making her cry out and rock against him. "Is that adrenaline from the bear?" he asked, teasing her with the words she'd given him. "Or for me?"

"Ha," she managed, then choked out a needy little whimper when he pushed up inside her, the sound meshing with the low, sexy rumble that came from deep in his throat.

His fingers held her still when she would have rocked, not letting her move. "Not yet," he whispered thickly, and stroked his thumb over her again, and then again, slowly increasing in rhythm and pressure, taking his cues from her reactions, which were shockingly earthy and base. "If you move," he managed in a low growl that she found sexy as hell, "I'm done."

She didn't care; in that moment she only cared about the way his fingers were moving on her, taking her places she hadn't been in so damn long, and then there was how he felt, thick and hot and big, God so big, inside of her. His hands were gentle and tender but there was something so raw about his every movement, so uncalculated, as if it had been as long for him as it had been for her. It had her nerves on high alert, leaving her so pleasure-taut, so unbearably sensitive, she was already on the very edge. She heard the whimper escape her throat, a horrifyingly embarrassing sound, but she couldn't stop or control herself.

With him, she could never control herself.

So she gave up trying. For this moment, she let herself go, just gave in to it, in to him, and her hands slapped on the hard floor on either side of his head. "Danny, now . . ."

Releasing her hips, he rose up to meet her, his hands sliding into her hair to bring her mouth to his.

Her permission to move.

So she moved. She rocked her hips, then again when he guided her into a rhythm that had her bursting wildly. Even more startling, he came with her. Simultaneous orgasm. It was amazing, soul-shaking, and revealing, almost too much so, and she tried to bury her nose into his throat, but he held her face, letting her see every single emotion as it hit him—the sheer, unadulterated desire, the hunger, the heat such as she'd never known, and perhaps the most devastatingly intimate emotion of all . . .

Affection.

And with his arms banded tight around her, holding on to her as if she was the most precious thing in his world, she stared back into his eyes and gave him the same.

Chapter 8

Well, holy shit, Danny thought as Hope flopped off him, gasping for breath.

From flat on his back on the floor of the shed, Danny did his own gasping for breath as he stared up at the ceiling. He couldn't have been more stunned if he'd just been hit head-on by a moving freight train. He'd just had the best sex of his entire life. On the ground. In the great outdoors. In the wilds of Colorado.

In the snow.

God, what he'd give to be able to shout it from the rooftops of all the assholes who'd ever given him a hard time in his school days for being the nerd.

Nerds unite.

Smiling helplessly, he rolled toward Hope. She had her pants on one leg, hanging off the other, her jacket half on and her top shoved up to her chin.

God, she was hot. And gorgeous. And sweet. And blurry. Where the hell were his glasses?

She'd flung an arm over her eyes, and was still breathing like she'd just run a marathon, which gave him a ridiculously dopey grin.

And the urge to nuzzle. Yeah, he wanted to draw things out, snuggle, cuddle, the whole bit. Maybe even go for round two. To that end, he scooted closer and slid a hand up her bare leg to her hip—

Sitting straight up, she pushed his hand away and began to right her clothing.

"Hey," he murmured, softly. "Are you—"

His shirt, the one she'd ripped off him only a few minutes before, hit him square in the face.

"Hurry," she said.

He pulled the shirt down. "Before the bear comes back?"

"Before someone decides to take a stroll and see us."

"In four feet of snow?"

"We're out here, aren't we?" She jammed her foot back into the one boot she'd managed to tear off. To hurry him along, she tossed his jacket over as well. "Why aren't you moving?"

"My bones dissolved. Hope, that was—"

"Fun," she agreed, not looking at him as she laced up her boot. "Thanks for that, I feel much better now. More relaxed."

"Okay, good, but—"

And while he was still stuttering, she stood up and walked off, her boots crunching in the snow as she went, muttering something about how that back door to the kitchen had better no longer be locked.

He lay back to resume his staring up at the ceiling, but something was under his ass.

His glasses.

He put them on his nose and sighed. They were bent to hell. "Thanks for that," he said, repeating Hope's words, then laughed at himself.

Something brushed his foot then, and picturing the bear, he leaped up, his pants still at his thighs—

And met the surprised gaze of one very curious deer, peering into the shed with huge doe eyes.

"Jesus," Danny said shakily.

Which was apparently too much for Bambi, and she took off, leaping like the picture of grace through the snow across the open yard.

Danny let out a breath and yanked up his pants—a guy needed balls of steel for this place. Giving himself a pep talk, including one about not letting himself think too hard about what he and Hope had just done—or how fast she'd run from it—he managed to get back to the B&B. He let himself in the kitchen door and came face-to-face with yet another audience.

Lori and Ben.

They were sitting on the counters sipping steaming coffee, but what he noticed most was their matching grins.

"Hey," Lori said sweetly.

"Hey." Danny looked out the window and saw to his relief that the shed was not visible from here. He turned and divided a look between husband and wife as he shrugged out of his jacket. "So I suppose neither of you know how Hope got locked out of here a few minutes ago."

"Um, what?"

"The door," he said. "It was locked."

"Huh." Ben lifted a shoulder. "Odd."

Lori nodded. "Odd."

He gave up and headed across the kitchen to the coffeepot. "I'm going to go check on the road conditions."

"Sure," Lori said. "But you might want to tie your left boot and rebutton your shirt."

He'd buttoned his shirt wrong. Perfect. He fixed that and bent to work on the boot.

"Must be a helluva wind out there."

Danny straightened and met Ben's steady, even gaze. Yeah.

It'd been a helluva wind all right, and its name had been Hope. "Do you happen to know if the roads have been cleared?"

"Yes, but it's going to be dark soon. You really going to head out?"

"Yeah." He needed to. Hope was a big girl, she'd made that clear. She didn't need nor want his help. And though she couldn't possibly deny the fact that she'd enjoyed their little outside tussle, he knew she was also over it.

Over him.

She'd be okay. She knew what she had to do to keep this place out of the clutches of her brother. He looked out the windows again. He told himself he was tired of wide-open skies and no skyline. Tired of the lack of Starbucks and no New York pizzeria.

But the truth was, the place had grown on him.

And so had Hope.

"Roads might be icy," Lori said gently. "And it's going to snow some more. We're awfully shorthanded. . . ."

"Well," he heard himself say. "If you're shorthanded . . ."

When Hope needed to avoid thinking about something, she'd found that nothing beat manual labor. To that end, she stood on the roof of the shed as the sun sank behind the mountains, shoveling the thick snow off the flat roof so it wouldn't collapse. She had the back floodlights on to see, and brain blessedly blank, was happy in her own little world, where there were no sexy nerds, no evil stepbrothers. . . .

Someone climbed up the ladder. A knit cap-covered head popped up.

Danny.

He tossed up a second shovel. "I know, you don't want my help. Too bad." With that, he climbed the rest of the way up, straightening with slow caution as he looked down at the ground. "Huh."

She raised a brow as he lost some of his color. "Afraid of heights?"

"No, of course not."

"Of course not," she repeated wryly when he sank to his knees and closed his eyes. "Okay, big guy. You just stay there, I'm nearly done here anyway."

"No. I'm going to help." Resolutely, he used the shovel to pull himself back upright.

Hope stared at him, feeling some more of those unwanted emotions clogging her throat. He was so different from any man she'd ever known. Loyal, intellectual, sharp-witted . . . and strong. So damn strong, from the inside out; strong of mind and character, strong of heart and soul, and that . . .

That was new for her.

He didn't care what people thought, didn't care about anything except doing the right thing, and damn if that wasn't the sexiest thing about him.

It was also more than just a little terrifying given what had happened the last few times she'd opened up and let someone in.

And in any case, she was strong, too. She reminded herself of this very fact as she resumed shoveling snow off the roof. She ran this place on her own and she'd find her own answers, without spending every single breathing moment thinking about what she'd done with Danny in this very shed.

But oh, good sweet Jesus. *What they'd done in this shed*. She couldn't help but think about it. Relive it. And think some more. Because . . .

Wow.

Genius Boy really had had the moves.

She tried to shake it off, tried to go back to the blessedly blank state, but she couldn't. The truth was, she'd managed to avoid thinking too much about her financial situation. She'd avoided thinking about the possibility of something happening to her perfect world out here in the Colorado boonies she loved so much.

But she couldn't keep that up. Things had to change.

Danny had gotten to his feet and was back-to-back with her, shoveling snow as steadily as she.

He was a rock.

A solid rock.

And if she followed his business ideas as well as her own, she knew she could make it. "Danny?"

Turning his head, he looked at her. Smiled. "Yeah?"

"You were right."

A slow smile curved his mouth. "Much as I like hearing that . . ." He straightened, stretched his back, then leaned on his shovel. "What am I right about—" He broke off when the shovel slid out from beneath him.

"Danny!" she cried as he slipped and the ice layered beneath the snow on the roof propelled him toward the edge of the roof.

"No!" Her heart leaped into her throat as she jumped forward to catch him, but the ice caught her, too.

And she went over with him.

Chapter 9

For the second time that day, Danny braced for his life to flash across his eyes.

It didn't.

That's because thanks to the sheer amount of snow they'd shoveled off the sides of the shed, he had a nice, cushy fall.

When he hit the huge berm of snow, he slowly sank in up to his nose. He spit out a mouthful of snow and was trying to figure out how to actually swim out when he was hit in the chest by . . .

Hope. He stared down at the bundle that had landed on him, his amusement at himself vanishing instantly. Heart in his throat, he pulled her in. "Are you—"

"Did I hurt you?" she demanded, getting herself out of the snow pile much faster and surer that he did. She ran her hands up his neck to cup his face. "Danny?"

Maybe it was evil of him but the sheer concern and worry in her eyes alleviated his fear, and in fact warmed him to his very frozen toes. As did the way they kept trying to rescue each other. He had no idea why that struck him so funny, but he loved it.

He'd never in a million years imagined getting stuck in Colorado. Or liking it. But there was real life out here, adventure in every single moment. Not the drudge of an office, or any office politics, but warmth and affection from the people he was coming to know, and an easy, simple joy in the chores to run the place, which were anything but simple—

"Danny," Hope said tightly, running her hands down his body, clearly checking him for broken bones.

It seemed certain things were becoming habit with him—a habit he could get used to.

"Talk to me," she demanded.

"If I told you where it hurt, would you—"

"Oh, God. Can you make it inside?" Without waiting for an answer, she slipped her arm around his waist and tried to take all his weight as she led him to the back door. "Almost there—"

"Hope, I was only kidding—"

She took him through the kitchen, down the hallway into her bedroom. She pulled him past her bed and into her bathroom. "You're icing up. Gotta get you out of those clothes."

"Hope—"

"Hold on." She cranked on the hot water and then turning back to him, tugged off his jacket, knit cap, gloves. But it wasn't until she dropped to her knees in front of him that his breath backed up in his throat.

"Lift up," she said, and he realized she'd untied his boots. Before he could say a word, she leaned past him to check the water temp. "Good," she said to herself.

Shaking his head on a low laugh, he reached down and pulled her up.

She immediately went to work on unbuttoning his shirt, but because the feel of her hands on him set him back about thirty IQ points, it took him a minute to say her name again.

By then she had his shirt off and her hands were at the zipper of his pants, except if she got them off, she wasn't going to find an injured man, but a hot, aroused one—

She shoved down his pants, then stared at his erection. "Well, hello there."

"Yeah. I'm not hurt, Hope."

"I'm beginning to get that," she murmured, still looking at the part of him that was the happiest to be naked, which pretty much waved hello at her. "Did you fall off that roof so I'd sleep with you again?"

"Ha—*Jesus*," he managed when she wrapped her hand around him and slowly stroked. "I—"

"Get in the shower, Danny." Letting go of him, Hope put a hand to his chest and pushed him toward the steaming shower. Then she pulled off her shirt.

Never one to argue with a woman who was stripping, he took a step back into the water, not taking his eyes off her as she discarded her boots, unzipped her jeans, and shimmied out of them.

Gaze locked on his, she unhooked her bra, wriggled out of her panties, and then stepped into the shower.

"Look at you," he whispered against her mouth, pleasure suffusing him as their now-wet bodies slid up against each other. "You're so beautiful, Hope."

"So are you. Who'd have thought it, but I can't keep my hands off you, Genius Boy."

With the hot water raining over them, Hope moved her hands to his face, so close he could feel her gentle breath on his skin. "This is nice," she whispered.

Nice. It was, but he hoped to hell he could do better than *nice*. Hope's breasts were against his chest, her belly and thighs flush to his, pressing her back against the wall to free up his hands, which he skimmed up her body.

Her breath came out in a whoosh, and she melted against him. "I like it when you take charge," she murmured.

"Yeah?"

"Oh, yeah."

"Then turn around."

"Um . . . what?"

Hands on her hips, he twisted her around so that she was now facing the wall.

"Danny—"

"Shh." He pressed his lips to the nape of her neck, loving how she shivered as he took his mouth on a cruise downward, over the slim arch of her spine, to the sweetest ass known to man. He kissed the backs of her thighs, and then in between, urging her legs open so he could take her over the edge, which she let him do with ego-stroking ease. God. *God,* he thought as she came for him with some more of those sexy helpless little whimpers she made in the throes. He didn't want this to be just a hot weekend affair.

Not when for him it was already so, *so* much more.

Still breathing heavily, she turned around to face him again, pulling him up to kiss his jaw, his throat, whatever she could reach, her mouth telling him that he was the best thing to happen to her since sliced bread, and he could have told her that it was the same for him. This, with her, was the rightest thing in his life. Her arms were wrapped tightly around him, so tightly he could scarcely breathe, and he didn't care. Closing his eyes, he bent closer and tried to breathe her in as he lost himself in her. "Hope . . ."

"This is crazy, right? How much we want each other."

"I know something even crazier." He cupped her face. "How I feel about you. Hope, I—"

She yanked his mouth back to hers, kissing him deaf, blind, and dumb. Waaaay back in some dim recess of his mind he understood that she wasn't ready to hear his feelings, but then she wrapped her legs around his waist so that he could enter her. "I have three condoms left," she whispered in his ear just before she lightly sank her teeth into his earlobe.

Jesus. Three condoms sounded about right, but damn if he'd rush through this, even for her. Gripping her hips, he pressed her hard to the wall as he kissed his way down her body. The under curve of a breast. A rib. Her belly. A thigh.

Between.

"Again?" she murmured shakily, trembling with excitement.

Oh, yeah, again. "Open for me," he murmured against her, and when she spread her legs, he stroked his thumb over her. With a soft cry, she slid her fingers into his hair to hold on, so gorgeous standing there on quivering legs, the steaming water running down her tight, toned curves. Her nipples were hard, her chest rising and falling with her quickened breathing. She shifted restlessly, opening her legs even more, and he took her in, all pink and glistening for him. He nearly came from that alone as he leaned in—

"Danny," she choked out, tightening her fingers in his hair as his tongue made a slow, torturous pass over her flesh. *"Please."*

Yeah. He'd most definitely please. He'd please her, and then himself, and then hopefully start all over again until neither of them could move. Opening her a little more, he gently sucked her into his mouth and kept sucking in tune to her breathy sighs, the sounds of which drove him a little crazy as he slid a finger into her and drove her to the very edge, then straight off it.

The sight of her coming again was one he knew would highlight his fantasies for the rest of his life, and as her knees gave out, he caught her against him. Reaching out of the shower for her jeans, he found the condoms, then using the wall as leverage, thrust into her.

She revved up fast to join him, which was a good thing because with her mouth racing over his face, his jaw, with his name tumbling from her lips in that sexy breathless little pant of hers, with her fingers embedded into his ass cheeks trying to urge him on faster, harder, more, more, more, he wasn't going to last. "Hope—"

She burst again. Or still. He didn't know, but it catapulted him right into an orgasm so intense his toes curled. He completely lost himself as he spent into her, slapping a hand to the wall behind her so that they wouldn't fall. Instead they sank together in a slow, tangled heap right there on the shower floor, with the now tepid water raining down on them.

"Wow." That was all she said, in a dazed, dreamy voice that made him smile. "Wow . . ."

They toweled off. Hope bent for the pile of clothes, and several folded up papers fell out of his jacket pocket, papers he'd meant to show her after they shoveled off the roof. She gathered them up for him, going still as her eyes took in his research and the tentative offer he'd drawn up. He'd hoped to try to buy the lot from her, but that hadn't felt right. This place was hers. So instead he'd planned to lend her the money she needed to pay off Edward.

"What's this?" she asked, a veil coming down over her face.

"A way out of your problem."

"I've already told you I can handle this."

"You're going to lose the B&B, Hope. And it's wrong. You don't need to—"

"Did you have this planned all along?" she asked in a very quiet voice. "You and Edward?"

"Of course not."

"I think you did." She slapped the papers to his chest. "I think you planned this all along. Maybe you didn't really quit."

He stared at her as what she said sank in. "I did quit, Hope. Do you really think I'd—"

"Yes! God, I'm so stupid!" She slapped her own forehead. "Of course you didn't really give up what must have been a solid six-figure salary to start over."

"Careful," he said softly. "You're sounding a lot like that rat bastard you hate so much."

"Is that right? And how exactly does Edward sound?"

"Honestly? A bit pig-headed."

"Pig-headed," she repeated on a mirthless laugh. "Oh, honey. I haven't even gotten started." Buck-ass naked, she walked to the door.

"Where are you going?"

"To call Ben so he can snowmobile you out to your car."

"Hope—"

"Don't." And still buck-ass naked, she walked right out of his life.

Chapter 10

"You're a stubborn-ass fool, Hope."

Hope stared in disbelief at Lori. They stood in the kitchen, squared off at the island. "Um, excuse me," she said very carefully. "But I don't think you heard me correctly."

"Oh, I heard you. Danny came here to—"

"—take my business."

"To check on his boss's investment," Lori corrected. "And instead of being a stubborn-ass fool—like a *certain* person I know—he adapted. He worked his tail off for us, even going over and beyond to help you research alternatives, including offering you a personal loan to buy you both time and financial freedom. You know what, Hope? You're right. He's a bastard."

Hope let out a breath and turned to Ben, who was suited up in his snow gear, with his snowmobile just out the door ready to take Danny back to his car.

As she'd asked. "Maybe you could talk some sense into your wife, Ben."

And Ben, sweet, kind, wonderful Ben who *always* had Hope's

back, shook his head. "Not this time, baby. I'm sorry. But my wife has a point."

"Goddammit. You're just saying that because you sleep with her."

He smiled, warm and sure. "Well, there is that. But face it, the guy hasn't done a thing except try to help you, Hope."

"He came here—"

"Because of his job. And yet once he arrived, in fact from the *moment* he arrived, he did nothing but try to help. Problem is, you don't do help, do you?"

He didn't mean it as a jab. She knew that, but it felt like a red hot stab of a poker in her gut just the same because *dammit*. Was she really that person? Was she that much like Edward? Since she didn't like the answer to that question, she closed her eyes, and when she opened them again, Danny had come into the room, jacket on, duffel bag over his shoulder. He moved to hug and kiss Lori good-bye, then turned to Hope. "January first," he said solemnly. "And don't mistake my softness for his. He won't be soft if you don't pay. You know that."

"You're not soft," she whispered.

He looked at her for a long moment but said nothing, and then turned and nodded to Ben. They both went out into the dark, stormy night, where the wind and snow battled to come in until the kitchen door shut.

Closing them out.

The cold didn't leave Hope, though, and she wrapped her arms around herself. She felt her eyes swim, and knew the truth. Danny was right. Lori and Ben were right. "Okay, fine. I'm a stubborn ass who's far too much like the family I resent with all my heart."

"Yes," Lori agreed mercilessly. "You are."

Hope choked out a laugh as outside she heard the snowmobile

rev and take off. Her heart did the exact same. "No!" She went running out the door to stop Danny from leaving, and—

Plowed him over into the snow.

They landed hard with him on the bottom.

"Oh, my God, I'm sorry!" she cried. "Did I hurt you?"

"No—" He hissed out a breath when she cupped his face with her snowy hands. "Your hands are cold."

"I'm sorry." But she didn't take her hands off him. She couldn't. She didn't want to take her eyes off him, either. "You aren't even gone, Danny, and I miss you."

His eyes seemed to glow behind his glasses. "You . . . miss me?"

"Yeah."

"But . . . you asked me to leave."

She sat up and pulled him up with her, keeping her hands on him, noticing with a heavy heart that he didn't do the same. "You didn't."

"No."

"Why?"

He looked at her, his glasses fogged and wet with snow. "First tell me why you came running out of the kitchen like a bat out of hell when you thought I'd left."

Heart pounding in her ears, she gently pulled off his glasses and cleaned them on her sweatshirt, then replaced them, relieved to see his warm eyes were still warm.

And on her.

"I was wrong," she whispered, glad Ben was gone and that Lori hadn't followed her out. She wanted to be alone, no audience for this one. "Really wrong."

He nodded agreeably. "About anything in particular?"

She stared at him and had to laugh. Wasn't that just like him to sit there in the snowstorm patiently waiting for her to get her words together? "About getting scared and sending you away."

"So . . . now you're not scared?"

"I've taken my time letting a guy in before, and gotten *royally* screwed. Maybe the answer is in trying something different this time. *Someone* different." She shook her head at his silence. "Okay, I'm not making sense. Look, the important thing to note here is . . . I'm over myself."

"Good. So when were you under yourself?"

She looked into his smiling eyes and felt her own helpless smile curve her lips. "I've never been good with asking for help, Danny."

"You didn't ask. I offered."

"Turning it down was instinctive," she admitted. "I wanted to handle things on my own."

"Understandable." He reached for her hand, and just like that, the fist around her heart, the one that had been there so long she'd forgotten what it was like to take a full breath, released. "So back to my change in tactic," she whispered, her voice rough with emotion. "I want your help—not your money. I can't take your money, but—"

"Hope—"

"I mean, I want you, Danny. Your brain, your sense of humor, your incredible roof-shoveling skills . . ."

His next smile came slow and sure, and he pulled her in for a hug that warmed her from the inside out. "Seems fitting," he said. "Since I want you, too, temperamental stubbornness and all."

She pulled back to look into his face, feeling her relieved-smile face. "So . . . I don't suppose you get to Colorado often."

"There's no CPA in town, did you know that?"

"I guess I never noticed." She found that her throat was tight, almost too tight to talk. "You'd really be happy here?"

"I think it's the company," he said with a serious nod. "Though it might be the bears and frozen pipes."

God, his smile. "Danny."

"It's you, Hope. It's all you." He squeezed her hand, running his thumb over her knuckles. "But there's something you should know." He brought her hand up to his mouth. "I'm falling for you. Hard and fast."

"You—" She let out a breath and touched his jaw. "Really?"

"Yeah. So what do you say, are you going to go out with me when I move here?"

A bone-deep warmth filled her. "I think I could clear my schedule now and again."

"Good." He slid a strand of hair behind her ear and smiled into her eyes. "You asked why I didn't leave. It's because I asked you to accept my help, without first telling you how much you've helped me."

"Come on. I didn't help you with anything."

"Yes, you did. You made me remember to feel for something other than just work, to feel something with my entire heart and soul."

Emotion welled up and threatened her air supply. "That's convenient," she managed. "Because my heart and soul seem to want to be with yours."

His eyes were shiny, so damn shiny she couldn't look away. "The best Christmas present I've ever had," he murmured, and leaned in and kissed her, giving *her* the best Christmas present *she'd* ever had—him.

Ms. Humbug

Chapter 1

Three days before Christmas, City Planner Cami Bennett looked at her reflection in the Town Hall employee bathroom mirror and gave herself the silent pep talk. *You can do this. You can do something besides work your tail off. In fact, having fun is just like work, only . . . better.*

Probably.

Oh, who was she kidding? She liked the big O's—order and organization.

Orgasms would have been a nice addition to that list, but due to being a little uptight—and, okay, *a lot* anal—those kinds of O's were few and far between.

Now the big city hall annual Christmas party was later tonight, a masked ball where "fun would be had by all," and she was required to go.

Oh, goodie.

It wasn't that she was the female equivalent of Scrooge, but more that everyone at work always seemed to go on and on about the holiday ad nauseum—decorations, gifts, travel plans. Somehow, they'd all built themselves personal lives as well as careers, something Cami hadn't managed to do, and Christmastime just emphasized the failure on her part. She hated the pressure of the parties, the expense of buying her family gifts they didn't need or want, and, most especially, the loneliness.

Until now she hadn't had much time to think about it, not with the huge town shake-up that had involved the mayor and his very pretty boyfriend's private sex tapes being stolen and posted on the Internet for perusal by anyone with $29.95. It'd been the biggest scandal Blue Eagle had seen in decades, and no one yet knew how the rest of the town's staff was going to fare when all the cards finished falling.

Especially since the now-*ex*-mayor's boyfriend had turned out to be two weeks shy of legal age *and* the son of the D.A.

Ouch.

The front page of the *Sierra Daily* had showed a picture of Tom Roberts, stripped of his mayor's title, being led out of his office in handcuffs.

Talk about airing your dirty laundry in public.

A couple of councilmen had been dragged through the mud as well, one with a paternity scandal and the other with a bank scandal. Both accusations looked false, but were ugly nevertheless.

Morale had never been lower in Blue Eagle.

A soft sound came from one of the bathroom stalls, a sort of . . . mewl. "Excuse me," Cami said to the closed door. "Are you okay?"

The only answer was a whimper.

Concerned, Cami moved closer. "Do you need help?"

"Oh, God. *Yes!*"

Cami bent down and looked beneath the stall. She could see a pair of Jimmy Choo black toeless pumps, the ones Cami had drooled over in Nordstrom's but had not bought, choosing instead to pay her mortgage for the month.

Facing the opposite direction of the Choos was a pair of

men's black leather dress shoes, equally expensive, and Cami went still. She knew a man who wore shoes like that. Ned Kitridge. He was a city councilman, and her casual date for the past two months.

Embarrassment warred with fury.

Fury won.

Before her eyes, the woman's pumps lifted off the floor and vanished. There was a thunk against the stall door, and a long female sigh of pleasure.

And then the sound of a zipper.

In shock, Cami watched as an empty condom packet hit the floor.

Steaming, horrified, she staggered back. Even the bathroom was seeing more action than she.

And with Ned, *Ned,* a man who hadn't made a move on her, not once in six dates!

As her ego hit the floor next to the condom wrapper, Cami grabbed her purse and exited the bathroom, nearly blinded by an unhealthy mix of anger and mortification. But could she just slam out of the building? *No.* She couldn't abandon her compulsive, organized, anal routine. Hating that she couldn't, she meticulously shut off her adding machine and the light over her drawing board, glancing at the new sticky note on her computer.

Cami,
  I need to talk to you before the ball. Meet me in the conference room at 7:45.

Ned

Yeah, she just bet he needed to talk to her! Only a few moments ago, she had assumed—hoped—he'd actually pick her up at her place so they could go to the ball together. For eight weeks now, he'd driven her crazy with his need to take things slow. Slower than a-snail's-pace slow. Slower than icicles-melting slow. So-slow-she'd-been-losing-interest slow.

And yet in that bathroom, he hadn't seemed to be taking anything slow.

Don't think about it.

The others on her planning team—Adam, Ed, and Lucy, usually all too happy when things were going bad for her—had told her to be patient with Ned because he was a great guy.

Well, Ms. Choos apparently thought so, too. Damn it, even more than tearing Ned apart, she wanted some sexual action.

She wanted the man-induced orgasm.

As she left the building, steam coming out of her ears, she didn't see another soul. This deep into the year, the nights fell early in the Sierras. In pitch blackness, she made her way through the parking lot, the icy air cooling her off. With a few hours before she had to be back for the dreaded Christmas ball, she should hit downtown and knock off the list of gifts she needed in order to make a showing at her parents' house for Christmas dinner.

After all, she hated an undone to-do list.

But she was too shaken from the Ned-screwing-in-the-bathroom scene to stop. Plus, it was snowing lightly, just enough to dust all the windows on her car, hampering her vision. She pulled out her ice scraper from beneath her driver's seat and attacked her windows, but the ice stuck stubbornly. Giving up, she got into her frozen car and cranked the heater, which fogged the windows, adding to the visibility challenge. Things kept getting better and better. Forced to roll down her window to see, she stuck out her head.

But the falling snow blocked her view. So did her own iced-over car. Damn it. She put the car into reverse and slowly eased off the brake—*wait.*

Had she seen movement back there?

Again she stuck her head out the window, but all she could

see was snow flurries. Hell. Luckily, she knew she was the only one in the lot, so with another light touch on the gas, she crept out of the parking space and—

Crunch.

Oh, God! Oh, damn! Jerking her car into park, she leapt out of the car with her heart in her throat and came nose to nose with a man—scratch that. Nose to broad chest. "I'm *so* sorry!" she said, trying to blink the white flakes from her eyes to see past the man's long dark coat and hood. "I—"

"You weren't looking."

"I couldn't see—"

"I honked."

"I'm sorry—"

"Are you in *that* much of a hurry to get to the Christmas ball?" he asked.

It suddenly sank through her agitation that she knew that frustrated male voice. Craning her head back, she lifted her gaze past broad shoulders and stared up into a pair of slate-gray eyes filled with annoyance.

Oh, no. *No, no, no.*

Not him. Anyone else on the planet but *him.*

The *him* in question pushed back his hood, his dark hair glistening with snowflakes, making him seem even more fiercely intense and devastatingly handsome, if that were possible. Cami imagined even the most hardened of women would sigh over those chiseled features and that rock-hard body.

But not her. Nope, she was entirely unmoved.

Because in addition to the fact that he stood on her last nerve, he was the newly appointed mayor.

Her boss.

Her nemesis, Councilman Matt Tarino. They'd worked together in planning for two years before he'd moved on to councilman six months ago, and in their time together, they'd done nothing but gone head-to-head. He was the bane of her existence.

And now he was mayor. That he was tough as nails and cowed to no one when it came to getting fair share and equal housing for the lower-income population—her pet project—didn't matter. Nor did the fact that he'd been an excellent city planner, an advocate for all that she herself fought for.

Not when he was everything her orderly, organized, rule-loving brain couldn't fathom. He had no patience for precedence, rules, or expectations, and adding insult to injury, he seemed like sin personified, possessing a charismatic presence that conquered worlds, parted seas—and women's legs—with a simple smile.

It drove her crazy.

Logically she knew that these feelings were coming from the little fat kid inside of her, the one guys used to cruelly call Whale-Tail, but she didn't care. He was just far too perfect. Everything about him made her want to gnash her teeth into powder.

And now, Merry Christmas to her, because she'd crunched his front fender and taken out his right headlight, and quite possibly ruined her life and her career—which *was* her life. Closing her eyes briefly, she opened them again and looked anywhere but into Matt Tarino's frustrated face. That's when her gaze landed on his feet.

Specifically, his black leather dress shoes.

Not Ned in the bathroom with Ms. Fabulous Choos, but . . . *Matt*?

And just like that, her humiliation vanished, and so did the ball of nerves lodged in her throat. "It was *you*," she breathed. "You were the one in the women's bathroom!"

He blinked. Snowflakes fell from his long, dark lashes. "What?"

It made perfect sense. Women were always talking about him, sighing over him, drooling over him . . . "I heard you two in the stall," she said in disgust, crossing her arms. "Now, I'm sorry I ran into you, but truthfully, you'd distracted me. Get a room next time, sheesh!"

A slow shake of his head. "I can assure you, I don't frequent the women's bathroom."

She didn't believe him, of course, but his denial did mean that she had to take full responsibility for her own stupidity. Damn, she hated that. Sighing, she rubbed her temples. "Okay, fine. You're being discreet. I get it. I'm sorry about your headlight. I'll have it fixed. Just let me get my insurance information—" She turned toward her car, but he took her arm and pulled her back around.

He was always doing that—*that* being whatever he wanted. In fact, she figured if she looked up "alpha male" in the dictionary, she'd find his picture there.

"You're looking like a Popsicle," he said. "It can wait until tomorrow."

Unexpected decency. That, too, made her self-righteousness difficult to maintain. She wished he'd be an ass about this, but even she had to admit that while Matt defined stubbornness and mule-headedness, he also possessed integrity in spades. She'd seen it in action, when he ran town meetings, maintaining the voice of reason, even if it had a sarcastic edge.

She also knew him to be wild, daring, and a complete rebel at heart. So much so that no woman had ever tamed him.

Cami had never even considered trying, especially since she was too competitive to give him the upper hand, in or out of bed.

After all, he was unlike any man she'd ever been with, or wanted to be with—not that she had much to go on. He was just a little uncivilized, just a little politically incorrect. Not afraid of a battle.

And she so wanted to say *not* decent.

But he was still holding onto her arm, guiding her off the icy asphalt and into her car.

"Matt?" The female voice came from the pretty blonde sticking her head out of the passenger side of his car. "What's taking so long?"

Cami rolled her eyes and muttered beneath her breath to Matt. "Probably you should have stayed in the women's bathroom."

"Her car wouldn't start. I'm giving her a ride home."

"And don't forget the ride in the bathroom."

"I wasn't in the bath—"

"Whatever." She tried to pull her door shut, but his big body was in the way.

"Are you going to be careful?" he asked.

"Move, or lose a body part."

"Just don't hit reverse until I get out of your way," he said with a smirk, wisely stepping out of her way just as she slammed the door.

Chapter 2

Matt's evening could be going better. He could be at his brother's house nursing a beer and a pizza while watching the Lakers game.

Instead, he had to forgo his favorite evening wear—jeans—for a tux. In less than half an hour, he was going to be standing around, smiling at ridiculous small talk about the weather, eating tiny little hors d'oeuvres of questionable origin that never filled him up, all while being scrutinized by every single guest there, even by people who'd known him for years.

This was because he had a big old bull's-eye on his back, courtesy of getting the mayoral position unelected.

Never mind that there had been a city hall vote that he'd won by a vast majority. Never mind that he'd never done anything but great things for the town of Blue Eagle. Never mind that he was exactly where he wanted to be—for now—when it came to work.

Until he figured out who the hell was messing with the town's reputation, there would be rumors and doubts and questions. Frustrated over that, he left his house. Still snowing, which meant good skiing this weekend. The roads would be icy. Not so good. He got into his car and headed back to Town Hall for the ball. His starched shirt scratched him every time he so much as leaned forward to adjust the radio. His shoes were making his feet unhappy campers.

And a mile from his house, the rest of his headlight fell out. Nice, and yet the irritation faded as he remembered what Cami's face had looked like when she'd realized she'd hit *his* car.

Frazzled.

The thought made him grin because Cami frazzled was an amusing sight. A sexy one, too. It was her eyes, so brave, so huge and expressive, that made him inexplicably hungry, and not just for melting chocolate.

But more than just her eyes got to him. She had one of those bodies that women complained about and men loved, curvy and lush despite the yoga she did with her team for relaxation—useless in her case because she was incapable of relaxing, he'd discovered.

In fact, it was the office joke—she was so tightly wound, she squeaked when she walked.

Most men would be put off by that, and given her dating record, they had been put off but good. But he had a feeling that beneath all the organization and planning and general analness beat a wildly passionate heart. He saw it when she was lost in a project at work, when she stood in front of the council and argued for that project with all her might. How many times had she made it her personal goal to pit herself against him for any of a million reasons?

And each and every time, the air between them had crackled like lightning.

The truth was, whether she admitted it out loud or not, they'd been dancing around the sexual issue for two years. She was an amazing opponent, sharp and intelligent, ruthless, with a single line of focus that he'd seen in only one other person.

Himself.

Beyond that, they were polar opposites, she with her love of order and rules, he with his utter disdain of both. And yet somehow they'd made an incredible pair, and during their two years of mutual city planning, they'd improved the quality of life in Blue Eagle and its growth rate more than any other team in the city's history. It was something to be proud of, and he was.

But he'd moved into the council now, and they no longer worked side by side. In fact, she worked for him, a phenomenon he was quite certain drove her crazy.

And made him grin some more.

He pulled back into the parking lot and looked at Town Hall. The building had been built in 1890 and was, in fact, an historical monument. It had once been an icehouse, a storage unit in the days before refrigeration. Truckloads of ice had been shipped from here to San Francisco on demand. It'd been renovated three times since, and now white lights were strung across the front, anchored by groups of holly and pine branches, backlit by the bulbs. In front, on either side of the walkway, were small Christmas trees, decorated earlier in the week by the local elementary school children.

At the sight, some of Matt's spirit picked back up. So he was in a tux. So he'd have to drink champagne instead of beer. So he was going to miss time with his brother watching the game. Things were pretty darn good for him, and he was thankful. He'd go inside, smile and make merry, and maybe even figure out who was wreaking all the havoc for the town staff members. Not that Matt condoned the ex-mayor's crime of seducing minors, but whoever had exposed Tom, as well as lodged the accusations against the two councilmen, had done so publicly for a reason.

Someone was having a grand old time screwing with the town council.

Turning off his engine, he reached for the required mask. It was black, with an elastic string to go around the back of his head so he wouldn't have to hold it up to his face all night. Putting it on, he stepped out of the car and into the falling snow. Inside, the decorations were overly festive, bordering on gaudy, but that might have been due more to the badly played rendition of "Jingle Bells" coming from the high school band.

The room was already filled with staffers dressed to the hilt in their Christmas finery, all wearing masks, some elaborate, some looking like Tonto.

Mostly guys looking like Tonto.

Matt thought he saw Ed and Adam from his old team in planning. Couldn't miss Ed's carrottop or Adam's double-fisted drink habit. Plus they both waved, so he waved back, and grabbed a flute of champagne from a passing waiter.

"Matty," murmured a soft feminine voice from behind him. Turning, he came face-to-face with a woman in a tiny, sparkly silver dress and mask. Hannah Pelinski. He'd dated her once and had been put off by her relentless pursuit of a diamond ring. He smiled at her but tried to keep moving, only she started dancing right in front of him, blocking his way.

"Join me," she coaxed, making sure her breast brushed his chest.

"I'm sorry, Hannah. I have to . . ." Do anything rather than see the desperation in your eyes. "Go upstairs for a sec."

"Well, find me when you come back down."

He smiled rather than lie, and as quickly as he could, moved across the large room, past the elevators, to the stairwell, which was dark. Having worked in this building for so long, he could find his office blindfolded, so he didn't flip on any lights as he made his escape. On the second-floor landing, he turned left.

Halfway down the hall, he heard a soft thud. So he wasn't the only lurker tonight. He caught a flash up ahead, coming from the conference room, where there was a long wall of file cabinets, filled with years and years of information on everything from town council meetings to amendments to the city plan. Matt had no idea what, or if anything, someone would want from those files after hours, but as things had gotten crazy lately, he intended to find out.

He peeked into the dark room, smelling the pine of the small Christmas tree in the corner. The windows let in a glow from the string of lights on the outside eaves. He could make out the outline of a woman, sitting in the window well on the far side of the room. Knees up, her arms around them, she stared out into the night. Her dark hair was piled on top of her head, tendrils escaping along her neck. Her shoulders and arms were bared by her dress.

She didn't have on a mask, but even if she had, he'd have known it was Cami by the set of her narrow shoulders, as if they carried the weight of the world on them.

His little snooper had left a few file drawers open, some files sticking up. He was dying to know what had drawn her, what she was looking for, but felt even more curious about what was making her look so . . . sad.

She didn't look at him as he stepped into the room. "You're late," she said softly.

Was he? He glanced down at his watch. A quarter to eight. No, he wasn't late at all.

Which meant she was talking to someone else.

"Oh, Ned," she whispered, and hugged her knees tighter. "I need to talk to you, too."

Ned. *Ned?*

Still looking out the window, Cami stood. "I want to understand something."

Her profile was tight, grim. Unhappy. And suddenly he wanted to see her happy, even lost in laughter. Better yet, lost in passion, with him. He wanted her in his arms, his name on her lips.

"You like me, right?" she whispered.

Apparently more than he'd thought. "Yes."

"Then why don't you ever kiss me?"

Matt blinked. That hadn't been what he'd expected, though, in truth, he didn't know what he *had* expected. He knew she was talking to Ned, not to him, but he still stepped closer, so close that he could have bent his head and put his mouth to the nape of her neck. Her scent came to him, soft and lovely and incredibly sexy.

So sexy.

Her skin seemed to glow in the pale light. She tended to dress conservatively, and he supposed the cut of her black velvet dress was modest enough, but it molded and hugged her body, dipping both in the front and the back in a clean, sensual line.

"Ned?"

Christ, he wanted her to stop saying some other man's name. He wanted to hear *his* name.

She sighed then, a lost sound, a sorrowful sound, and unable to take it, he wrapped his fingers around her arm and turned her to face him. Before she could decipher the fact that he had a good four inches on Ned, he hauled her up against him and did as she'd asked. He kissed her.

Chapter 3

Cami sank immediately into the kiss. She couldn't see a thing in the dark room, but she didn't need to. Ned's mouth was firm yet warm, and tasted yummy. Then his tongue touched hers, and a bolt of desire zinged her from her roots to her toes, hitting all the good spots in the middle.

Oh, did he know how to kiss. Thankfully. She'd been worried because not once had he swept her up in his arms like this, against his body, inhaling her as if she was the greatest thing since sliced bread, and she loved it. Loved also the obvious hunger and passion he had bottled up.

For her.

Not to mention the delicious hardness of his chest, his belly, his thighs . . . in between. *God.* She hadn't been kissed like this since . . . she couldn't remember.

It didn't matter, she was being kissed now, and she couldn't believe how amazing it felt. Her bones melted, along with her reservations about Ned being the right one for her, and she ran her hands up his chest, winding her arms around his neck to pull his head even closer to hers.

His hands moved, too, at first grazing up and down her back in a seductive motion that drew her in even closer, molding her body to his. Up and down, farther each time, over the skin bared by her dress, until he cupped her bottom. The intimate touch shocked her, and aroused her beyond belief. He squeezed, the thin material of her dress and her new thong the only things separating his hand from her flesh. A brave departure for her, but she'd needed something drastic tonight, had needed to try something different. She'd loved the way she looked when she'd caught her reflection in the mirror. Sophisticated and glamorous—so unlike her usual self.

Now she was glad she'd dared, though his fingers on her, with so little barrier, felt shocking. One hand left her bottom, gliding back up her body to sink into her hair, dislodging a few carefully placed pins as he palmed her head, holding her in place while he decimated her with a kiss so deep and sensually charged, she could only whimper and let him take her where he would.

"Mmm," rumbled from deep in his throat, the hand still on her bottom urging her closer, rocking the softest part of her to the hardest part of him. Oh, God, this felt good, so good. If she let herself think, she might have admitted it was difficult to reconcile this deep, wet, hot, shocking erotic connection with the mild-mannered Ned, the one who was so nice and kind he often let people walk all over him rather than face a disagreement or handle a contradiction.

But she didn't think, because the rough growl that reverberated from deep in his throat made her weak. So did his sure and talented mouth, his steady and knowledgeable hands, both of which were driving her crazy. So did his mouth as it made its way to her jaw to nibble her throat. In fact, she had to clutch at him to remain standing. "You feel good."

In an odd reaction, he went completely still for a beat, then pulled back and stared down at her, the mask covering the upper part of his face but not the heavy rise and fall of his chest as he breathed erratically.

That's when it hit her. Ned wasn't this tall. Or broad. Or built.

Then she caught the glittering of his eyes.

Not dark brown, but . . . steely, stormy gray.

Oh, my God.

Not Ned. Not Ned, but—Reaching up, way up, she grabbed his mask. She wasn't tall enough to yank it off over his head, so she pulled it down and stared into those glittering eyes. *"You."*

"Me," Matt agreed utterly without repentance or apology.

Stepping back in horrified, humiliated shock, she came up against the window just as his mask, caught by its elastic string, slapped him in the chin.

Without a word, he ripped the thing off and stepped toward her.

"Don't," she choked out, her every nerve ending still pulsing with hopeful pleasure. She lifted a hand to hold him off, but he just took her fingers in his and came up against her, trapping her between the window and his body.

The window was icy cold. But not Matt. Nope, his hard body radiated heat and strength as he cupped her jaw until she was looking him right in the eyes. "Well, *that* took me by surprise," he murmured.

"What are you talking about? You knew exactly who you were kissing!"

"Yeah, but I didn't expect to be leveled flat by it."

"You expect me to believe that *you* were laid flat? *You,* the man who's kissed every single woman in a hundred-mile radius?" God, she was a fool. She'd known better, a small part of her had known from the moment he'd touched his mouth to hers—Ned would never have taken her like that, kissing hard and deep and unapologetically fierce—but her body had surged with such heat and need, and a desire so strong, she was still shaking from it.

And yet, the pathetic truth was, Matt had just been playing with her. It burned, she could admit, and burned deeply. All her life, she'd been the outcast. She'd been a chunky, nonathletic, clumsy kid in a house full of lean, coordinated, beautiful people. She hadn't improved much as a teenager, and though her frenetic exercise and dieting had finally worked, leaving her much fitter now, the stigma had never left her. Inside, she was still the left-out, laughed-at, fat kid, the girl who was the object of a wager among the boys of the varsity basketball team—the winner was to be the first boy who could get a pair of her "granny panties" to hang as a prize in their locker room—the woman who even now men tended to keep their distance from.

The remembered humiliation still burned.

She heard the footsteps coming and turned toward the doorway just as another man appeared, also in a tux. Mask in hand.

Ned.

And in that flash, from a distance of twenty-five feet or more, Cami wondered how she could have ever mistaken the two men. Ned wasn't as tall or built as Matt, instead a comfortable height for looking straight into his eyes, a nonthreatening bulk that brought to mind a scholar rather than a tough boxer or basketball player, as Matt's physique did.

And that wasn't the only difference between them.

There was the fact that the nice, kind, sweet Ned would never have taken advantage of a dark night and a mask, kissing a woman simply because the opportunity presented itself.

"Sorry I'm late," he said, and moved into the room, eyeing Matt inquisitively. "Tarino."

"Kitridge." Matt turned back to Cami. "Enjoy the ball."

Enjoy the ball? She'd enjoy kicking his butt, that's what she'd enjoy, but before she could tell him, he was gone.

When they were alone, Ned smiled curiously at her but, true to form, didn't ask. There was no reason why that should annoy the hell out of her, but it did. Her dress was wrinkled across the front where she'd been mashed against Matt, her hair was half up and half down thanks to his busy fingers, her mouth was still wet from his.

And Ned didn't appear to think anything of it. Frustrated, she grabbed her mask from the window seat and went to move past him, noticing that his tux was wrinkled, too—sort of endearing, really—and that his shoes—

Oh, my God.

His shoes were still black leather, identical to the ones Matt had worn, and still identical to the ones in the bathroom stall from earlier. Lifting her gaze to Ned's face, she was further disconcerted to find him blushing slightly. His usually perfectly groomed hair was standing up on end, and he still wasn't meeting her eyes. "You're late," she said slowly. "But you're never late. You're wrinkled, but you're never wrinkled. You're blushing, your hair is a mess . . ." She stared into his guilty eyes. "It *was* you in the bathroom. You've been making out with someone else."

Ned shifted from one foot to the other, jamming his hands into his pockets. "Technically, it's not someone *else*, if you and I have never made out."

"But . . ." No, she refused to ask why not her, why it was never her.

"I'm so sorry." His voice was rough with the apology she hadn't gotten from Matt. "I didn't want to hurt you."

"Wait." She couldn't think. Funny how her brain could work on an entire city plan, formulating for population and roads and more, and yet now, here, she couldn't process a thought. This wasn't supposed to happen this way. *He* was the office geek. *She* was the prize here!

"Cami, *Jesus.*" He squirmed. "I don't know what to say. It's just that you . . ." He lifted a shoulder. "You scare me."

"What?"

"And Belinda—"

"Belinda. Belinda Roberts?" The daughter of the ex-mayor and a city mail clerk? Who was still in college and giggled when a guy so much as looked at her?

"She's sweet and caring," Ned said defensively.

Which, apparently, Cami was not.

"She makes me cookies," he said. "Oatmeal raisin, because of my cholesterol."

Cami could have done that. Probably. If she'd even known he had cholesterol issues.

And if she'd known how to work her oven.

"She doesn't argue or disagree with me at work," Ned said. "Or make me feel as if my ideas are stupid."

"I don't—" But she did. She couldn't help it. Many of his ideas *were* stupid. And she had little to no tolerance for stupidity.

"I'm really sorry," he said again, softly, with surprising thoughtfulness. "I really didn't intend for you to find out like this. I wanted to come here and talk to you like adults."

"Right," she said. "Because *adult* is screwing the file clerk in the women's bathroom."

"Again, very sorry." He looked desperate for a change of subject. "I intended to tell you tonight, but then I found you in here with Matt. What did he want anyway?"

"Uh . . ." *Ms. Pot, meet Mr. Kettle.* "Nothing." If *nothing* meant the hottest, wildest kiss she'd ever experienced.

"Okay, then. Well . . ." More shuffling, this time accompanied by a longing look at the door. "I hope this isn't going to be awkward."

She just laughed.

Ned's flush lit up the dark. "You look really great tonight. Your dress—"

"You can go now, Ned."

"Thank you." In a cowardly blink he was gone.

Men. Cami kicked a file cabinet closed as she left.

It turned out Cami was grateful for the masked part of the ball after all—who'd have thought—because it allowed her to stay virtually "hidden" for the hour she forced herself to stay and smile and make nice. Trying to forget the kiss, she danced with Adam and Ed from her department, and she danced with eager-beaver Russ from the Permit Department, though surely her feet would never recover. She danced with a few others as well, mostly because it meant less talking.

And then she made her escape, leaving the festivities that had been meant to boost everyone's low morale. She drove home reliving the mortifying portion of the evening. In her quiet condo, she decided to grow from the experience. And then she buried herself in the work she'd brought home because, as it turned out, work was all she had.

The next morning, she went into her office early, and to protect herself, she put a sign on her door that said STAY OUT OR DIE.

But apparently the new mayor couldn't read because half an hour later, Matt stuck his head in, wearing one of those wicked smiles that had always annoyed her in the past but that now inexplicably scraped at a spot low in her belly.

"Hey," he said. "Busy?"

Just looking at him reminded her of last night. Of his bone-melting, heart-stopping kiss. Of how he'd held her as if he could do nothing else. How he'd gotten hard and rocked her hips to his. She'd dreamed about that part in particular, damn it, and remembering brought the heat to her face. She shouldn't be picturing the mayor with a hard-on. She especially shouldn't get hard nipples at picturing the mayor with a hard-on. "If I say yes, I'm busy, will you go far, far away?"

His grin spread.

Good God, could the guy be any more gorgeous? Or annoying? Or sexier? Now it wasn't just her nipples going happy, but things were happening between her thighs, too. "Didn't you read the sign?"

"Yes." He pulled a pen out of his pocket. Clicked it on. Eyed her with a mischievous lecherousness.

"Don't even think about it," she warned, gritting her teeth when he underlined the STAY OUT part. Then shut the door—with him on the wrong side.

He smiled.

She did not. But she wanted to, damn him, so she got up, walked around her desk, and reopened the door, silently inviting him to leave.

"Ah," he said. "Someone forgot to eat her Wheaties this morning."

"And someone forgot he was an ass—"

"Still mad, I see." He nodded as if this was perfectly acceptable to him. "How long do you plan on pouting?"

She gaped. "I am not pouting. I never pout."

"Then what's this?" He rubbed his thumb over her lower lip, which was indeed thrust out petulantly.

The touch electrified her, and she struggled with her reaction. If his expression went smug, she was going to have to kill him.

But he didn't look smug at all. He looked as shocked as she felt.

In the startled silence, a woman walked by her office. Danielle was a city clerk but looked like a stripper, and when she saw Matt, she stopped and smiled. "Hey there, big guy. Nice dancing with you last night." She made some promises with her bedroom eyes and body language before moving on.

"Big guy?" Cami shook her head. "Never mind, I don't want to know. Please just go away."

"Yeah." He looked at her for a long moment. "But only because I have three meetings, all scheduled at the same time."

"I'm in two of them with you. Oh, and I hope *you* ate *your* Wheaties because at the first one, for the proposed amendments to the town plan? I'm planning on nailing you."

His eyes heated. "Promise?"

She felt her insides quiver at his expression. "Get out."

"Okay, but first I wanted to talk to you about last night."

"No. No way."

"I had some trouble sleeping," he said, all kidding aside. "I was thinking maybe you did, too."

"Slept like a baby." Yeah, if babies had wet dreams.

"You slept like a baby," he repeated.

"You betcha."

He didn't believe her. "Then why are you in such a big hurry to get rid of me?"

"Because I don't like you."

He grinned. "Liar."

"Oh, just get out!" To make sure that he did, she shoved him, then closed the door firmly on his grinning face.

She felt her own reluctant smile and was just glad she'd shut the door before he could see it. The last thing she needed to do was egg him on.

"You still there?" he asked through the door.

"Where else would I be?"

"Just wondering if you've managed to bite back your smile yet."

She threw her pen at the door, then rolled her eyes at his soft laugh.

The next day, the local newspaper broke a story on one of the public officials in the Public Works Department. It turned out the official had once been charged with extortion in Florida, a charge no one here had known about.

The article went on to raise the question of whether such a thing could happen right here in Blue Eagle.

The official resigned, leaving everyone in every department

unsettled and nervous. Cami's haven—work—had become a nightmare.

In a hastily called meeting, Matt stood before all of them, cool and calm, effectively outlining a plan of attack to face the public and an inner plan of attack to find out what the hell was going on. Afterward, he stayed around talking in his easy way, making everything seem okay, when Cami knew it wasn't.

She had to admire how he handled himself, how he eased everyone's mind with just a few words. Which didn't explain why she didn't feel eased, but . . . revved. Every time she inadvertently caught his eyes, her body hummed and zipped, like it had when he'd touched her. She was a walking-talking live wire, and any minute now she was going to snap. It was hard to maintain her composure like that, but she was the master of control, so she managed to fake it.

After the meeting, she stood in the break room, waiting for the coffee to brew, ignoring the mistletoe some poor sap had hung over the doorway in hopes of getting lucky. To keep her hands busy, she was compulsively straightening up, putting the filters and mugs in their places, refilling the pitcher of drinking water on the counter. Not that it would all stay that way, but the motions calmed her. Organizing always did.

It was the kiss that was unnerving her, she knew that. Just thinking about it infuriated her because there were so many other things to be obsessing over—the newest scandal, the fact that there were only two shopping days left until Christmas, that she didn't have a boyfriend to shop for . . .

She poured herself coffee and stood there stirring it, wishing things could be different. But Matt had only been playing with her, she *knew* that. She must have just imagined how good it'd been, how hot—

"I could show you again."

With a gasp, she lifted her head and looked into Matt's amused, aroused eyes.

"Yeah," he told her. "You said it out loud."

Groaning in embarrassment, she brought her hands up to her hot cheeks, but he pulled them away. "Don't," he said in that voice that Cami was certain could coax a nun out of her virginity. "Let me show you that you didn't imagine a thing."

"No. No way."

"Okay, then." His hands slid to her hips, and her body quivered hopefully. "Then how about *you* prove *me* wrong?" he murmured, and pulled her close.

Chapter 4

It was sick of him, he knew, but Matt loved the way he could shake Cami's composure. Loved even more the way she shoved her nose so high in the air she became in danger of getting a nosebleed.

"Don't be ridiculous," she said in a frosty voice he was coming to realize meant her control was slipping as well. The interesting thing was she didn't push him away. "I'm not going to kiss you again just to prove there's nothing between us." She added a laugh that didn't fool him any more than her voice had. "We're grown-ups. We're professionals. We're—"

"Hot for each other," he said.

When she only glared at him, he laughed. "You know I'm right. Come on, admit it. You're dying to kiss me again. You're thinking about it. Hell, you're talking to yourself about it—"

"I am not going to dignify that with a response."

Leaning in until their noses nearly touched, he grinned right into her eyes. "I double-dog dare you."

"Please," she said with a sniff. "I don't feel the need to take every single dare that comes my way."

"Then I win by default."

Steam nearly came out of her ears at that, which was fun, too. So was the sparkle of life in her eyes. Never mind that it was an angry sparkle—he liked it. He liked her.

A lot, as he was discovering.

Then, the break room door opened. Adam walked in, took one look at the two of them in such close proximity, and raised a brow as he reached for a mug. "I didn't realize you two guys were knocking it out."

Matt went from amused to pissed, and so did Cami by the looks of her.

"Probably it's why you approved Cami's open-space amendment for North's Landing," Adam said, oblivious. "Too bad I don't have a vagina, or I could get my own agenda passed, too."

Before Matt could say a word past the red haze now blocking his vision, Cami stepped toe-to-toe with Adam, tipping her head back to glare into his eyes. "Watch out," she said very quietly. "Your knuckles are dragging."

Adam snorted as he walked past her and sat at the employee lunch table. "All I'm doing is calling it like it is. Now I know all I have to do is sleep with Matt."

Matt took a step toward him, not exactly sure what he was planning on doing, but his fingers itched to encircle Adam's neck. Cami beat him to it, picking up the pitcher of water on the counter and emptying it into Adam's lap.

Adam yelped and surged to his feet, doing the cold-water-in-the-crotch dance.

Cami shot a glare toward Matt, making him very grateful he hadn't been the one to place the last straw on her back. Then she swept from the room.

Matt leaned back against the counter, arms crossed, watching Adam yell and swear and hop around like an idiot.

"Uptight bitch," Adam griped, sagging back to the chair. "My balls are wet."

"Adam?"

"Yeah?"

"If you ever pull anything like that again, insinuating that Cami is anything less than a lady, or that I'd accept bribes, you won't have any balls to worry about."

Later, Matt worked his way through the stacks upon stacks of work on his desk, trying to prioritize the various fires. When he looked up again, he realized the hallway was dark, the place silent.

It was nearly eight o'clock.

So much for getting a couple of ski runs in before dark. The cons of his new job he knew. His time was not going to be his own for the remaining portion of his term. But after that, when he'd made his mark, when he'd done what he wanted to do for the town, he could happily walk away. Sure, he was only thirty-five, but that was the beauty of retiring young—he'd be able to enjoy it.

He and his brother had had it planned since their wild and crazy and completely uncontrolled childhood. There was much about that time that they didn't want to ever revisit, but one thing they agreed on—the freedom had been great. Eventually they would get back to that, using their winter days to ski themselves stupid and the summer days to travel, or whatever suited them, but Matt couldn't get there until he worked out the mess here—

In the utter silence of the building came an odd scraping.

Matt left his office and walked the dark hall, looking for the source of the sound. The receptionist's desk was shaped like a half circle, with a wall of filing cabinets behind it. The computer was dark, as was the little fake Christmas tree with more lights than faux branches that Alice had in the corner. Everything looked completely normal . . . except that the chair moved slightly, the wheels squeaking against the plastic runner.

Only no one was in the chair.

Matt came around the half circle of the desk and stopped short.

"There's a good explanation for this," Cami said from her perch on the floor beneath the desk.

Matt leaned a hip against the wood and casually crossed his arms. "Really."

"Yeah." Staring up at him, she bit her lower lip, her mind no doubt whirling.

She wore a black-and-white-checked wool skirt and white silk tank top. Earlier she'd had on the matching checked jacket, but it was gone now. Her skirt had risen high on a pale, smooth thigh, her tank snug to her most lovely curves. He'd noticed the outfit earlier in the day because her black heels had been so sexy he hadn't been able to take his eyes off them, or her legs. Or any part of her, for that matter. She was such a delicious contradiction, so tense and uptight about work, and yet there were these little hints of a wildly passionate side.

He wanted to see more of it.

"Would you believe I lost an earring?" she asked, coming up to her knees. She wasn't wearing those sexy heels at the moment.

Was it him, or had her nipples just gotten hard, pressing against the thin material of her tank? "You never lose anything."

"Well, then . . . I forgot to get my phone messages earlier."

"You *purposely* forgot to get your phone messages."

"Fine." She blew a strand of hair out of her face. "I came to leave a message for Alice."

"Let's try something new," he suggested, still leaning casually against the desk. "Like the truth."

A sigh fluttered out of her lips. "I'm snooping."

"For?"

"For the same thing you're interested in—finding out which

206 / Jill Shalvis

one of us is trying to screw up Blue Eagle's reputation beyond repair, and why."

Pushing away from the desk, he crouched in front of her. On her knees, staring up at him, it struck him how unintentionally erotic her position seemed. "How do I know it's not you?" he asked.

Her eyes were clear and right on his. "The same way I know it's not you."

That surprised him. "I figured I was at the top of your list."

"I know you better than that," she said.

"Really? What do you know about me?"

"That you're incredibly cocky." She sighed. "But you're good at what you do, damn it, so you get away with it. And that's not a compliment," she said, pointing at him. She sighed again. "I suppose it can also be said that you have a code of honor. You don't cheat. It's why you never have just one woman in your life. If you did, you'd have to give up all the others." She lifted a shoulder. "You can be trusted."

"Thank you," he said wryly. "I think."

She lifted her shoulder again and then began to crawl past him.

He grabbed her ankle. "For the record," he said when she looked back at him. "It's not that I can't deal with only one woman at a time, but that the right woman hasn't come along."

She snorted and crawled free of the desk, then stood up and walked off.

Matt took the time to enjoy the sight of her nicely rounded ass before following her. He was struck by how petite she was without her shoes. She barely came to his shoulder.

She didn't appear to notice the discrepancy when she stopped, turned, and poked him in the chest. "Who are you looking at?"

"You."

Her eyes narrowed. "Why?"

"Ever look in the mirror? You're not so bad to look at."

She stared at him, then shook her head. "I don't have time for your lines. I want to be home before midnight." With that, she wheeled away, moving down the dark hall again, her bare feet silent, her hips swinging gently, mesmerizing him with her attitude and utterly accidental sexiness.

"Why do you have to be home before midnight?" he asked.

"I'll turn into a pumpkin. Here." She entered the mail room. "I was thinking maybe someone is reading incoming mail."

"There's only one mail clerk."

"Belinda," she muttered.

"She's young, but awfully sweet. I don't think—"

"If she's so sweet, then why aren't *you* dating her? Why aren't *you* doing her inside a women's bathroom stall?"

He eyed her carefully. "You keep mentioning the women's bathroom."

She sighed, rubbing her temples. "You know what? Never mind."

"No, I think I want to hear this."

She strode over to the mail sorter's desk and the computer there. Someone had forgotten to turn off the radio, and "Santa Claus Is Coming to Town" strained lightly over the airwaves. Cami's hair was wild now, from her own fingers, and he loved the way she walked, full of authority and temper, her ass tight and tempting.

"I walked in on her having a fun time in the bathroom," she said, booting up Belinda's computer and chewing on a nail while she waited, silent and stewing.

He also loved watching her sizzle, but this was more, there was sadness, too, and he moved closer. "Fun. You mean sex?"

"I just never thought he had it in him—" Computer booted, she began clicking on the keys, but something in her tone had him taking her arm, pulling her up and around to face him.

"I don't want to talk about it," she said, looking at a spot somewhere over his shoulder.

Cupping her jaw, he waited until her eyes met his. And in them he found his answers. "*Ned*," he said softly. "That asshole."

"Yes, well, you're right about that," she said in a lofty tone that didn't fool him one bit. He remembered the night of the party. She'd thought he was Ned. She'd asked him why he never kissed her.

And now she was doubting herself. "You are far too good for him, Cami."

"Really? Then why does no one else want to date me either? Why do I have to beg men to kiss me? Oh, forget it—Oof—" she said when he tugged her back against his chest.

"I do not want a pity kiss," she choked out, hands flat on his pecs.

"That's good, because you're not getting one." With one hand anchored low on her spine, the other slid into her hair at her nape. Watching her, he lowered his head. "This is the real thing," he murmured.

"Matt . . ."

"Shh." When their mouths connected, he felt it reverberate through him. Like coming home, he thought.

With a surprised murmur, she pressed even closer, tentatively touching her tongue to his. He lost it. Growling low in his throat, he dug in, losing himself in the feel and taste of her, pulling back only when she put her hands against his chest and pushed.

He stared down at her, and she stared right back, not trying to break free, just breathing like a lunatic and blinking those huge, expressive eyes at him, as if coming awake from a long sleep. "I don't think—"

"Perfect. Don't think." And he took her mouth again, savoring her soft little whimper of pleasure and the way she fisted

her hands on his shirt, anchoring him close. He had no idea
how long they went at it this time before they had to stop again
to breathe. He'd pressed her back against the desk, and had one
hand on her sweet ass, the other toying with the strap of her
tank top, a muscled thigh shoved between her softer, more giving ones. Her nipples were boring holes into his chest, and he
was so hard he couldn't see straight. "God, you look good
here."

"In the mail room?"

"In my arms."

"I don't need pretty words, Matt. I'm not the kind of woman
a man fusses over."

"Then you've been with the wrong men."

"Agreed."

He looked down into her flushed face. Her lips were full,
and still wet from his. Her eyes were luminous, and shining
with so much emotion she took his breath. "I could be the right
man," he said quietly.

She laughed, then her smile faded when he didn't laugh back.
"You're . . . not kidding."

"No." This wasn't just play, or just a kiss. This wasn't just
lust, although he felt plenty of that right this very minute.

It was the real thing.

But she shook her head. She didn't believe him. Hell, he
couldn't blame her, given his life and the way he'd lived it—one
day and one woman at a time. He wouldn't have believed him
either. "I want to be with you," he said, and though it might
have sounded rash, it wasn't. It'd been building for a long time.
"Exclusively."

"What?" She shook her head, as if certain she'd heard him
wrong. "What does that mean?"

"You might have heard of it. It's called dating."

She gave him a long look. "I wasn't under the impression
that you understood the word *exclusive.*"

"I understand more than you think." He kissed her just beneath her ear, enjoying the way she clutched at him and shivered. "Watch out, I just might convince you to believe in this. In me."

"Don't hold your breath." Pushing away now, she turned to the computer. Then, after a moment, she glanced back at him, looking uncertain. "What I'm going to do here is a bit of an invasion of privacy. You might want to go home and pretend you never saw me here tonight."

"You're going to look through people's e-mail files. Specifically, the e-mails sent to the newspaper."

"Yes."

"You really think someone is stupid enough not to have deleted the correspondence?"

"I'm banking on it."

He smiled. "E-mail files here at the city offices are public records. So technically, there's no invasion of privacy, because there is no privacy. Scoot over."

She looked surprised. "It might take a while."

"I realize that, Sherlock."

"Don't you have a date or something?"

"Two things, Cami. One, not all men are scum. Two, I just told you I wanted to date *you*. And only you."

She never took her eyes off him as she absorbed his words, looking so bewildered. And so heartbreakingly unsure, as if no one had ever made her such a promise.

Hell, he'd never made such a promise himself. *He* should be the terrified one. And there was some of that, but also an inexplicable sense of hope. "Scoot over," he said again, gently.

After a moment's consideration, she made room for him at her side. Just where he wanted to be.

Chapter 5

By two A.M. they'd gotten through half the offices and had found something both shocking and morbidly interesting. There wasn't just one employee e-mailing information to the newspaper, but a spattering of them, none from the same department, and none who had any obvious connections to each other.

Was everyone in this building losing their minds?

They were missing something big here, Cami knew it, and because she did, she refused to give up.

Oddly enough, so did Matt. He'd benefited from what had happened to the town council more than anyone. He'd become mayor because of it. It would be further to his benefit to leave it all alone.

And yet he stayed, brow furrowed in concentration, fingers clicking across the keyboards as fast as her own, concentrating intently on everything they went through.

He was on her side.

They'd been on the same side before, and they'd been on opposite sides. He was a fierce competitor, she knew this.

And also fiercely loyal.

The combination, the dichotomy of him, fascinated her, when she didn't want to be fascinated.

And now he'd said he wanted to date her. Imagine that. She and Matt. The problem was, she *couldn't* imagine it. So she organized her thoughts like she did everything else and put them out of her way for now, to be obsessed about later. Far later.

Matt suggested they wait until they finished going through all the rest of the computers before making their findings known, which would take at least one more night, possibly two. They went to the employee break room for food, and Matt came up with a package of donuts. "Probably stale, but chocolate is chocolate."

Cami stared at the donuts, mouth watering as she went to war with her old fat self.

Eat them, that old fat self begged.

You might as well just spread them over your hips, sneered her new, thinner self.

"Split them with me?" He was already breaking into them, sending the scent of sugary sweet chocolate wafting across the room.

Her stomach growled. "Um . . ." *Get some control, woman.* "No, thanks."

"Sure?" He shoved one in his mouth and moaned unapologetically. His tongue darted out to catch a crumb off his lip. "Nothing like the rush of sugar at two in the morning."

He was smiling, his eyes filled with pleasure. He found pleasure in everything he did, whether it was working, laughing, arguing . . . She imagined he'd be like that in bed, too. Her belly tightened.

He caught her looking at him and smiled. "Change your mind?"

Had she? He was cocky, edgy, at times arrogant, and then there was the fact that she couldn't outwit him like she could most others. Which in effect meant she couldn't control him, or how she felt about him.

Just like she couldn't control the urge for donuts.

"Cami?"

"No, I haven't changed my mind. Not about anything."

Without looking too disturbed, he popped another donut into his mouth and brushed the sugar off his hands. "Your loss."

It didn't matter to him either way, she knew that. He'd probably already forgotten he'd said he wanted to date her. *Exclusively.* Men like him said stuff like that all the time just to get laid.

At least she hadn't fallen into that trap.

"You have a thing against stuff that's good for you?" he asked.

"The stuff you're referring to is *bad* for me."

"I wasn't talking about the donuts."

"Neither was I."

He laughed softly, and again the sound scraped at a spot low in her belly. "All work and no play . . ." he began.

"Makes me feel worthwhile."

"Do you ever let up on that self-control?" He looked genuinely curious. "Just to enjoy yourself?"

"I don't like to deviate from a plan."

"Don't I know it," he said with feeling, reminding her of all the times they'd gone head to head over one of her "plans."

"If I'm driving you so crazy, why are you here?" *Using words like exclusive?*

He stepped close. "Oh, you're most definitely driving me crazy."

"Then why—"

He put a finger to her lips, his touch making her heart race, reminding her how much her body craved him. "You're also making me feel things I haven't felt in a long time," he said. "I like you, Cami. A lot, I'm finding. Now, about deviating." He cupped her face. "Buckle in, because this is a big step off the planned path for the evening."

"Matt—"

He kissed her. It was another of those soul-deep connections that had her hands lifting of their own accord, anchoring her to him as her fingers dug into the hard muscles of his shoulders. A soft little murmur escaped her, horrifying in its dark neediness, but there it was. Undeniable.

She wanted this more than the donuts, and that was saying something. She held on tightly, purring in pleasure when his hands roamed up and down her back, squeezing her bottom, her hips, up to her breasts. His thumbs made a pass over her nipples, and when he found them hard, he let out a rough sound that rumbled from deep in his throat.

She let out a matching moan when she heard it, and the desperation behind it, and she pushed at him.

He lifted his head, looking hot and bothered and extremely sexy for it.

She staggered back against the refrigerator, feeling drugged. And achy, deliciously so. "That's . . ." Words failed, so she just fanned the air in front of her hot face.

He wasn't breathing any more steadily than she was. "I see what you mean about planning." His voice was husky and aroused. "If we'd planned that, maybe I wouldn't feel as if I've just been hit by a bus."

"There's no plan in the world that can prepare you for *that.*"

"Which proves that it's okay to wing it once in a while."

"I can't argue with you when my brain is fried." She poured herself a large, cold drink of water. It didn't cool her off. "I need to do something organized right now," she decided.

"Right now?"

"*Right now.*" She opened the drawer by the sink. A mess.

Perfect. She began to straighten the forks and spoons and pencils and matches, pulling out a Christmas CD that someone had shoved in and forgotten.

Matt leaned against the counter. "Let me get this straight. You can face the entire town council and argue a point until their eyes cross, but you can't face me?"

She stilled her fingers, hating her weaknesses. "You're right. I should do my own office first." She marched out of the break room and into her office. "Go home," she said when he followed her so closely she couldn't get her door shut without taking off his nose. "Get some sleep."

"I'd rather watch you organize your already perfectly organized office."

Jaw set, she went to her desk, pulling her top drawer open. Damn if every single thing wasn't already in place.

"So you're obsessive-compulsive as well as anal," he said conversationally.

"I organize when I'm nervous or upset. It's no big deal. I'm sure you do something for your nerves, too."

"Sure. Face the problem."

She whipped up her head, met his gaze.

"Talk to me," he said softly.

She looked down at the pencils and pens carefully set in their proper slots. She had one for erasers, too. And her tape. Her stapler. Everything was perfectly aligned.

"Cami."

In spite of his sincerity, she still hesitated. This wasn't an easy admission. "I used to be fat," she finally said. There. She said it out loud for the first time. "All throughout my childhood and school years. I was the fat kid in a fit, active, successful family. They were all perfect, and I wasn't." He wasn't running for the hills yet, so she went on. "Then I left home and went to college, out of the reach of my parents and brother and sister. I lost fifty pounds and got control of myself." She straightened her shoulders. "Being in charge and organized and controlling is who I am, and I realize you might see it as neurotic, but being this way makes me feel good about myself."

"You *should* feel good about yourself."

She didn't dare look at him or absorb his approval. "Once in a while I let myself relax, I let myself cheat. So I am warning you now, the next time you offer me donuts, be prepared to lose your fingers."

He didn't laugh or mock her. He didn't even smile. Instead, he stepped closer, lifting her chin with a finger. "We grew up in the same town, remember? I know how you used to be."

"You know I used to be fat?"

Now that finger traced her hairline. "I played basketball with your older brother. You came to the games."

Yes, she remembered. She'd stand at the concession stand and eat.

And eat.

"I don't care what you used to look like," he said softly, tucking a strand of hair behind her ear.

"Come on, Matt. Look at you. Your reflection probably sighs in bliss every morning. You're telling me appearances don't matter to you?"

"I'm telling you life experiences matter. Listen, my brother and I grew up with a teenaged mom who didn't know the first thing about being on her own, much less about raising two boys. We had no rules, no authority. Hell, we had no roof over our heads half the time. I worked damn hard to be who I am now, and I want someone who understands that, who has her own experiences to draw on. I want a woman who can talk to me, who can understand my world, who can be both serious *and* fun-loving. And if she just happens to be easy on the eyes, and believe me, you are extremely easy on the eyes, Cami, well then . . . lucky me."

She stared at him for signs of deception and saw nothing but open honesty in his gaze. "I don't know what to say to you. I think I should go home now." She turned off the lights.

Her office settled into darkness, but it wasn't complete. From the windows came the glow of the seasonal lights, twinkling merrily, casting shadows across the desk and floor.

Matt put his hands on her. She didn't protest as he drew her in. The soft night fell over them—hypnotic, lulling, sweetly silent—and when he touched his mouth to hers, she settled into the soft, gentle kiss.

"Night," he whispered, and stepping back, he slipped his hands into his pockets, leaving her wanting more, damn him.

The man was smart, she'd give him that, knowing when to push and when not to. If he'd kissed her senseless and then asked her to go home with him, would she have gone?

Of course not.

Oh, crap. She'd have gone in a heartbeat, and not because he kissed like heaven, but because he'd seen her at her compulsively organizing worst and hadn't gone running. Grabbing her purse, she made the mistake of turning back to him.

There was passion and heat swimming in his eyes, and something more—affection.

Oh, God, but that got her. How often did a man look at her like that? Never. How often did she feel this way, sort of quivery and . . . desperately horny?

Double never.

Maybe . . . maybe she needed a New Year's resolution—live life to its fullest, even if that means occasionally deviating off the known path. She could mark the deviating on her calendar for, say, once a month.

Starting now. She dropped her purse on her desk. "Matt?"

"Yeah?"

"Do you carry condoms?"

He blinked. "What?"

"I assume a man like you carries." She put her hands on his shoulders. "I've never made the first move before—"

"Cami—"

"Not because I'm a prude or anything, but because there's never been anyone I wanted badly enough to risk the rejection."

His eyes went dark, so very dark, as his hands came up to her waist. "I want to be clear, very clear," he said. "This is you coming onto me, right?"

"Yes." She swallowed hard. "It's a New Year's resolution sort of thing, a week early. Be kind, okay?"

"Cami, I plan on being everything you ever wanted." He lifted her against him and set her on the desk.

"Here?" she asked breathlessly, her heart in her throat, her body on high alert, beginning with her nipples and ending with a dampness between her thighs.

"Oh, yeah, *here.*" His big, warm hands settled on her thighs, pushing them open, and before she could decide how she felt about that, he stepped between them.

"Wait," she gasped.

He went still. "Really?"

Do it. Do *him.* "It's okay. It's a good kind of wait." Twisting around, she swept an arm across her meticulously neat desk, knocking everything to the floor in one fell swoop—her phone, her desk pad, her notes.

"Nicely done," he said approvingly.

She stared at the mess on the floor, chewing on her lower lip. The urge to pick it all back up nearly overpowered her.

Matt's mouth was solemn, but his eyes full of humor. "You want to take a moment and clean it up?"

That he'd read her mind so easily was a little disconcerting. "No, I'm . . . good."

He tipped up her chin, away from the mess. "Sure?"

"I want to be in the moment, damn it! Just once!"

"In the moment is just where I want you." His other hand slid down her spine to her bottom, tugging her closer.

Pressed up flush against him, she could feel every inch of him. He was hard, and it made her heart beat faster, heavier.

"Yeah, right here," he said softly, his mouth only a fraction of an inch from hers. "Just tell me if you need to stop to obsess about anything."

"No, I'm fine." Sort of. Pretty much. Oh, my God, he was big.

His smile was slow and warm and sexy. "Yeah, you're fine." And this time when he kissed her, she sank her fingers into his hair and kissed him back, thrilling to his firm, quietly demanding mouth, which stirred instincts long suppressed. Living life to the fullest. In the moment. *God, in the moment tasted good.* But there were too many barriers between them—his clothes, hers . . . Impatient, she pulled his shirt from his waistband, sliding her hands beneath to touch his heated skin, stroking up his smooth, sleek back, loving the feel of his muscles, bunched and tight. Letting out a little sigh of pleasure, she shifted to touch his flat abs, feeling him tremble. For her.

He knew her now, or he was starting to. He knew the real her, and he was still here, still wanting her. She could feel that wanting in his kiss, in the way he touched her, and the knowledge was so incredibly empowering and arousing, she gave herself up to it. To him.

She wasn't alone, not tonight, and marveling over that, too, she touched his mouth, feeling him smile beneath her fingers, his tense jaw, the muscles bunched beneath the wall of his chest. "I'm still fine," she marveled, giving him a breathless update.

He smiled and nibbled his way to her ear. She shivered, which he soothed away with his hands as he lifted her tank top. Looking into her eyes, he peeled the material over her head. Oh, God. Her inner fat girl surfaced for a brief flash.

He danced his hands from waist to ribs, palming her breasts. "Okay?" he murmured, his thumbs rasping over her nipples.

"O-okay," she managed. *Don't think about him seeing your body, don't think about it, just enjoy.*

"You're so beautiful," he said, banishing her inner fat girl for another day.

Somehow she stripped off his shirt as well, looking at him in the low light. The man had a body like a pagan god, and she wanted to touch it.

Before she could, he dipped his head, forging a path of hot, open-mouth kisses down her shoulder as he unhooked her bra, baring her breasts.

The heat within her spread. Fat girl stayed banished.

"Still okay?" he wanted to know as he bent to a breast. Licked. Sucked. *Bit.*

She panted for breath. *"Yes."*

"Good." His hands curled around the hem of her skirt, skimming it up her thighs. Then his fingers hooked into her panties.

She stared into his hungry eyes. "Um . . ."

"Tell me you're still hanging in," he said, his voice not so light now.

"Y-yes. Hanging in."

"Good. Now hold on." He stepped back, tugged, and her panties vanished. Cold air danced over her legs, but then he was back between her thighs. With his usual bluntness, he looked down at her sprawled out for him like some sort of feast, letting out a hungry sound she felt all the way to her womb.

Torn between the erotic sexual haze he'd trapped her in and a vulnerable embarrassment, she squeezed her eyes shut. Not as experienced as she'd have liked, she didn't know the protocol here, or what to do with her hands. He'd told her to hold on, so she gripped the edge of the desk for all she was worth, struggling to remain calm. Should she say something? Tell him she didn't often climax with a man because it was hard for her to give up her control? Or should she just smile sexily and fake it?

Or do what she was already doing, which was panting for air because she could hardly breathe.

He took the decision out of her hands when he sank to his knees and stroked his fingers over her.

Her body jerked in surprise, in pleasure.

"Shh," he murmured, and with another rough sound of hunger, leaned in and tasted her.

Reality had no chance then, no chance at all. At the first stroke of his tongue, she became incapable of smiling sexily, or even of blushing, incapable of doing anything except holding onto that desk and gasping for air between little whimpers of pleasure. Oh, God, this felt good, this felt *amazing.* She could actually—She was going to—"Matt!"

"I know. It's okay. Come for me, Cami."

When she did come—*exploded*—with a shocked, breathless cry, he murmured his approval and did it again.

Did *her* again.

"Oh, my God," she panted when she could speak. She was flat on her back, blinking at the bright stars dancing in her vision. "I think I've walked into the light."

His face appeared above her as he braced a hand on either side of her head. He wore a grin, albeit a tense one. "Those are the Christmas lights outside the window."

"Oh." She smiled sheepishly. "That was . . . holy cow. You have no idea."

"Been a while?"

"*You have no idea.* There's more, right?"

"Oh, yeah, there's more." He unzipped his pants, put on a condom from his wallet, a task most pleasurable to watch, Cami thought dimly, her brain not quite connected, her body still pulsing.

"Still with me?" he asked.

"So with you."

"Good." Draping her thighs over his forearms, Matt gripped her hips and slid home, filling her to bursting, a feeling intensified by the low, serrated sound of desire that ripped from deep in his throat.

She could feel her toes curl as he breathed her name in a husky, destroyed voice. *"Cami."*

She couldn't respond, because within a few strokes she was clutching at him, panting, whimpering. *Dying.* Between the delicious friction and the expression of need on his face alone, she flew high, trembling, quivering, suspended on the very edge, until with a rough, guttural groan, he shattered. He was still in its throes when she took the leap with him.

Again.

Chapter 6

Cami told herself that she was fine, that she'd escaped from the experience in her office with Matt relatively unscathed. She told herself that all the way home, and all the way through her hot shower, and all the way through the next three hours in her bed, until her alarm went off at six A.M.

Just a torrid affair, like she'd always wondered about.

The after part had been a little rough, she could admit now—the coming-home-alone part. Matt had wanted her to go to his place, but she'd been unable to fathom repeating the whole mind-blowing experience and then walking away.

Once had been hard enough.

When her snooze alarm went off again, she got up and dressed. *Christmas Eve.* Most people wouldn't be going into work, but she was going to. Dedication at its finest, she supposed.

And a telling way to hold at bay the memories from last night. Or the loneliness she knew would hit her any minute now. The Christmas loneliness. She could try to forget, she could try to pretend it didn't exist, but it always came.

She entered her office and stopped short at the sight of her desk. The scene of her indiscretion, so to speak. Her momentary lapse in good judgment. Last night, she'd straightened it all up, she'd had to, but she didn't need to see all her things on the floor to remember what Matt had done to her there.

Pulling out her chair, she sat down and tried not to look at the blotter, which now contained an imprint of her butt. She dug into work, feeling very mature for doing so, but by mid-afternoon, she gave up. She had to get out, or lose her mind, so she headed downtown, where she wandered the long row of art galleries and unique gift shops to find her last-minute family Christmas gifts. Determined to be chipper and in the spirit, she hit them all.

And found nothing for her picky parents or impossible-to-buy-for brother and sister.

All around her, the trees and streets were lit with seasonal lights. Each storefront had been decorated, and Christmas music and delicious scents surrounded her. So did people. Everywhere. Couples, families, friends . . . everyone talking and laughing and having a ball, all in the holiday spirit.

No one seemed to be alone.

Except her.

She ended up back at her car, arms empty. *Damn it.* Determined, she sat there waiting for the defroster to work, wracking her brain. Finally it came to her. Ski-lift tickets. Her parents would love the excuse to dust off their skis, and her siblings would think the present original and cool. Cami let out her first smile of the day, because she just might have hit upon the perfect gift *and* the perfect way to impress her impossible-to-impress family on Christmas morning.

Congratulating herself, she drove the seven miles out of town to Eagle Ski Resort. There she purchased the tickets, and had just put them in her purse when someone said in her ear, "Well, look at that. You tore yourself from work."

The last time she'd heard that voice, he'd been standing between her sprawled thighs whispering wicked-sexy-nothings to her. Turning, she faced one Matt Tarino, dressed in black board pants and jacket, wearing a Santa hat and aviator reflector sunglasses, and holding his snowboard. He should have looked ridiculous. Instead, he looked fun-loving and carefree, not to mention incredibly sure of himself, and sexy as hell for it. Belatedly, she remembered his brother owned this place, so of course he'd be here. Or, maybe not so belatedly. Maybe she'd known—hoped—to see him. Disconcerting thought. As she stood there staring at him, wondering at the odd ping in her belly—and between her thighs—two women skied by and sprayed Matt with powder from their skis, laughing uproariously, flirting with their smiles and eyes.

Cami dusted herself off, surreptitiously watching Matt as he waved back, turning down their offer to join them. Instead, he moved closer to Cami and brushed some powdery snow from her cheek. "So. What brings you here?"

Now that they'd had raw, wild, animal sex on her desk, he made her feel even more off balance than usual, and she was painfully hyperaware of his every move. Even her nipples were hard. It was ridiculous, and to counteract the phenomenon, she stopped looking at him. "I came by to purchase some lift tickets for my family for their Christmas gifts."

"Nice gifts."

Let's hope they think so.

"Enjoying your Christmas Eve?"

"Sure." Less than she would a cruise to the Bahamas, but more than, say, a root canal.

Matt shoved up his sunglasses to the front of his Santa hat. "You're looking pretty uptight for someone who's enjoying herself. Come join me for a few runs before the slopes close."

She looked down at her long maroon skirt and sweater. "I couldn't."

"What's your preference, skis or board?"

"Skis, but I'd planned on going back to the office to finish going through those computers—"

"I'll help you after."

"But I don't—"

He tugged her close. She stared resolutely at his chest.

"Was last night so awful, you can't even look me in the eyes?" he asked quietly.

Surprised, she lifted her head. "No. No," she said again into his rueful and, damn it, hurt gaze. "It was . . . well, you know what it was. It was incredible."

His eyes smoldered. "So let me show you another good time. On the slopes."

She looked at him for a long moment, because she knew herself. She was falling, and falling for a man—especially him, the one man to make her feel things, the one man to get inside her and care about her—was dangerous. It gave him all the power he needed to hurt her. Scary, scary stuff.

On the other hand, it was only a few runs on a ski hill, something that was shockingly tempting . . . "Maybe for a little while."

With a smile that melted her resolve and very nearly her precious control, he led her inside the small lodge. "My brother runs the show here," he said, waving at yet another group of women who called his name from across the large room. "I just help out when I can. We'll get you all set up."

The next thing she knew, he had her in borrowed gear and on skis from the demo shop. And then out on the slopes.

Having a ball.

Truthfully, much of her fun came from just watching Matt. The man was sheer poetry in motion, all clean lines and easy aggression, with a wild abandon that aroused her just looking at him. Who'd have thought such a sharp-witted, politically driven man could move like that?

After last night, she should have known.

She wondered what *he* thought of last night, but they didn't talk about it. They just took the slopes with an easy camaraderie and laughter and . . . fun, and by the time the lifts closed two hours later, she felt chilled to the bone but exhilarated. For a few hours, she'd been like the people she'd seen in town, not alone . . . happy.

"Thanks," she said when she'd turned her equipment back in and he'd put his board in his locker. "I really needed that."

Standing in the lodge, he stroked a strand of hair off her face and smiled. "You're cold. I have a cure for that, too."

"I think you've cured me enough."

"Come on, Cami. What's the worst that could happen?"

That he would offer to warm her up, maybe in his bed, and she might be just weak enough to let him. And then she might not want to ever leave.

"Do you trust me?" he asked.

She stared into his eyes. She'd seen them stormy and furious; she'd seen them soft and heated. They were somewhere in between now, filled with an honesty and affection that took her breath. Did she trust him? She knew she didn't want to. "I wouldn't follow you off a cliff, but at work . . . maybe I trust you there."

He laughed. "A start, I suppose. What about personally? Do you trust me outside of work?"

Back to that jumping-off-a-cliff thing. "That's more complicated."

"Ah." He nodded agreeably, then shook his head. "Why, exactly?"

"Well . . . you like women."

"I believe that's worked to your benefit."

She blushed. "You like *lots* of women."

"Yeah." His smile faded. "I suppose that's the rumor mill you're referring to. You know, a lot of that is exaggerated."

"How much of it?"

"What?"

"What percentage of all the women I've seen drooling over you is exaggerated?"

He paused. Considered carefully. Ran his tongue over his teeth.

"Thought so." She searched her purse for her keys.

He reached for her hands to still them. "Should I judge you for your past?"

"No, but I haven't slept with every single man in the free world."

"Neither have I," he said, and tried a grin. When she didn't return it, he sighed. Rubbed his jaw. "Okay, listen. I've had a good time with life so far. I'll admit that much. But I'm not afraid of commitment. Can you say the same?"

"Yes." Maybe.

Probably.

Fine. Commitment made her nervous, a fact that was undoubtedly tied to her need to control every little issue. But she'd like to think she wouldn't let that stand in the way of a real relationship.

"I really don't see the problem here," he said softly.

He wouldn't. "We're so fundamentally different."

"You mean you being uptight, anal, and overly organized?"

She crossed her arms. "I would think people would love that about me."

"Maybe I'll love you in spite of it."

She went utterly still. "What?"

"Not here," he decided. "We're not doing this here. Come on."

He led her back through the lodge, across the icy parking lot, to the far side of the property where a couple of cabins faced the mountain vista. There was a driveway between them, and in it sat a truck and Matt's Blazer.

"My brother's," he said, pointing to one cabin. "And mine," he added, pointing to the other, opening the door, revealing a small but lovely living room accented all in wood. One wall was all windows, overlooking a white-capped peak, and another was filled with a stone fireplace. He had a Christmas tree in the corner, tall and beautifully simple, with white lights and red bows, but somehow it held more holiday spirit than anything she'd seen.

His couch looked like an old favorite, overstuffed and well-used. A football lay on the floor, along with a pair of battered running shoes, a stack of newspapers toppled over, and a very neglected fern. Leaning against the far wall were several pairs of skis, two snowboards, and two pairs of boots. Warm and homey but definitely lived-in. Her fingers still itched to at least straighten the newspapers.

Or jump Matt.

"I'll start a fire," he said, putting an arm around her and pulling her in close to his big, warm body. "Come get comfortable."

She couldn't. Shouldn't.

"I promise not to bite." He rubbed his jaw to hers. "Unless you want me to."

"You've lost your mind." But she looked into his eyes and melted a little.

A lot.

It was official. He hadn't lost his mind—she'd lost hers.

Chapter 7

"I shouldn't come in," Cami said in a last-ditch effort to save herself. "You don't want casual company tonight. It's Christmas Eve." She stood in his foyer, uncertain, and desperately trying to hide it from him. "I'm sure you have better things to do."

He just looked at her with amusement and something more, seeming tall and sure and so damn sexy. "Tomorrow my brother and I are going to watch college football and exchange fond insults, but until then, I'm all yours."

Until then? She swallowed hard. She was attracted to him, so so *so* attracted, but deep inside she knew she might not be able to control that attraction if she let him touch her again.

"You're thinking waaaaay too hard," he said lightly, taking her hand as if to make sure she couldn't run off.

"Bad habit, thinking too hard." She took a deep breath and stepped into the living room. "I still want to go back to work and search the rest of the computers . . ."

"I know." He moved to the fireplace and lit the already laid-out fire. "Come closer to the heat."

She did so slowly, hugging herself tightly, throwing him a smile that she hoped seemed confident, not shaky.

He went into the kitchen. She heard him moving around, and her heart went into her throat. He was planning her seduction. Probably lighting candles, finding music, hunting up condoms.

Her thighs tightened.

Bad body. No more sex. She'd had her fling. She'd had her fun. Time to hunker down now—

He came back into the living room with cheese and salami and cut-up apples on a plate. She stared first at the food, and then at his face. "You're . . . feeding me?"

"It's dinnertime. I figured if I took the time to make something, you'd vanish on me. But we're going to need fuel if we're going back to the offices—"

"It's just that I—" She cleared her throat. "I thought you were going to try to seduce me."

"Oh, I plan to," he said easily. "Just not until after we work, or you won't relax. And I want you relaxed, Cami. Really relaxed."

She stared at him. "You actually understand me. I mean *really* understand me."

"I'm trying."

"Matt?"

"Yeah?"

The hell with it. She tugged him close and kissed him.

"Mmm," he said in surprised pleasure, but after a minute, he pulled back and pushed the food in front of her. "Eat. Then the office. And then, Cami, then this. I'm going to take you to bed. *Mine.*"

His. God. How bad off was she that she thrilled to that idea?

* * *

The offices were dark and chilled, but Cami turned determinedly toward the department they hadn't yet gone through—her own.

The first three computers were clean, including hers. One office left. She stood in the doorway and looked at Ned's desk.

"We're committing equal opportunity privacy invasion," Matt said quietly. "We have to look."

"Despite the Belinda fiasco, he wouldn't hurt anyone, not this way."

"Let's just be absolutely positive."

"Okay."

To Cami's utter shock, they found several e-mails addressed to the newspaper, in Ned's sent file, one of which suggested the fire chief of Blue Eagle might be an arsonist. "Oh, my God," she whispered, looking up into Matt's grim face. "It's him, too." She couldn't believe it, didn't know what to think.

"You all right?"

It just made no sense. But she was all right. What Ned did didn't reflect on her, didn't mean anything except that Ned was an ass. *She* was okay. She was really okay, and it'd all started with that New Year's resolution to go for it, to deviate from the plan once in a while. To live life to its fullest . . .

And Matt was it. He was her "go for it," her "step off the path."

He was the way to live life to its fullest. And not just a one-time deal. "Matt?"

At her soft, extremely serious tone, he stroked a strand of hair from her face. "What is it?"

"Maybe you should sit down," she said a little shakily. "This is going to be a doozy—"

The office door creaked open behind them, and someone stopped in surprise at the sight of them.

"Hey," Matt said, but the figure standing there whirled to run.

"Shit." Matt surged up, just barely snagging the person by the back of the jacket.

Cami leaped for the light switch, then gasped in shock when the fluorescent bulbs sputtered to life and she found a gun in her face.

"Belinda," Cami gasped.

Belinda tore free of Matt's grip. Tall and willowy, with her long blond hair piled on top of her head, she was wearing black, studious-looking glasses and a tight red suit, none of which hid her beach-babe figure. "You two scared me to death," she said. "What are you doing in here?"

"How about we talk about the gun first?" Matt asked, gesturing carefully to the weapon still in Belinda's hand.

Belinda looked at it, flushed, but didn't lower it. "You scared me. I thought you were a burglar. I was just protecting myself."

"Well, it's just us," Matt said. "So you can put it down."

The gun wavered slightly, but remained cocked and aimed, now at Matt's face. "Why are you snooping in Ned's computer?"

Matt didn't so much as look at Cami as he slowly turned toward the computer in question. Belinda's aim followed.

"We were looking through everyone's e-mail files," Matt said.

Belinda didn't look happy as she followed him to the computer. "Why?"

"We were looking for the person leaking those vicious rumors."

"They aren't rumors if they're true," Belinda said, leaning in to read the screen. "And it was all true, no matter what anyone says."

"Really?" Matt's fingers flew over the keyboard as he turned his body completely away from Cami now.

So did Belinda.

He was turning Belinda away from Cami. Trying to keep her safe. *Oh, my God.*

"How do you know it was all true?" Matt asked Belinda.

Belinda stared at him.

He stared right back, calm and cool, despite the gun only inches from his face.

"You already know," Belinda guessed softly. "Don't you?"

"What, that you were the one who did the e-mailing from all those different computers?" Matt nodded. "Yeah. Just figured that out. So now what, Belinda? Because up until right now, you haven't committed a crime that would land you some serious jail time. The gun changes that."

Belinda looked at the gun.

"Don't be stupid," Matt said softly.

Cami felt frantic. The foolish man was baiting her! Heart in her throat, she took a step toward the wall, where Ned had plans of his latest pet project, a bike trail along the river. They were rolled up in a canister and weighed a good ten pounds. Hoisting them up, she took a slow step toward Belinda's back.

"What were you trying to do?" Matt asked Belinda. "You got your own father kicked out of here."

"He deserved it! He was cheating on my mom. With a *guy.*" Belinda shuddered. "And everyone here acted so self-righteous about it."

"So you hurt them, too?"

"Yes! And maybe you were next."

Matt shook his head. "You couldn't have gotten me, Belinda."

"Why not?"

"Because I'm smarter than you are."

Cami couldn't believe it! Didn't he see the gun right in his face? She could scarcely breathe for fear it'd go off by accident.

Belinda's hand wavered, probably with rage. Jesus. Cami took another step and raised the tube of plans. Matt looked up, and so did Belinda, at the same time lifting the gun, just as Cami closed her eyes and brought the plans down on Belinda's forearm, hard.

The gun flew into the air, then hit the floor, and with a frustrated, rage-filled howl, Belinda whipped around to face Cami.

"I figure I just saved you a long prison visit," Cami said. "You can thank me later."

Belinda let out an enraged scream and took a step toward her, but instead of strangling her, as Cami half-braced for, Belinda ran out of the office.

Matt strode to Cami and hauled her against him. Tense with fear and fury, he ran his searing eyes over her. "Are you all right?"

He was looking at her as if she was his entire world. She loved that. She loved him. "Of course I'm all right. You were the one with the gun in your face, you stupid, stupid man!" She tugged his face down and kissed him. "Hell of a time to realize I love you. We have to go after her."

He gripped her arms, lifted her up to her toes. "What?"

"I said we have to go after her—"

"The other thing."

"Later." She was shaking. "We have to—"

"Say it," he demanded.

"I love you."

He leaned in and kissed her, one hard, warm connection. "I love you, too. So damn much."

The words filled her, warmed her. She was in shock. And she was in love. Heady combination.

"I wanted to be your hero," he said. "But you saved yourself."

She ran her hands up his chest, feeling his heart pounding beneath her fingers. It steadied her. *He* steadied her. "It's okay. It's all part of that New Year's resolution. I'm going for it, remember? At all times."

"But you always go for it."

"At work, yes. But I'm expanding to other areas. Like my personal life."

His eyes shined with emotion. "You going for me, Cami?"

"Yeah, I guess I am. How does that feel, Mr. Mayor?"

He glanced at his watch. Two minutes past midnight. "Like the best Christmas present I've ever had." And he pulled her close.

Don't miss AUSSIE RULES by Jill Shalvis, available now!

Please read on for an excerpt.

It's fair to say that gutsy pilot Mel Anderson is happier in the air than on the ground. But she also has to clean up after her disorganized best friend and business partner and keep an eye on their employees, who tend to make more work than they get done. Now, the one man she hoped she'd never see again is back and looking for trouble. The kind of trouble that keeps Mel grounded in a most unexpectedly pleasurable way. . . .

Bo Black wants his family's airport back, and he's determined to get it. He might be a laid-back Aussie, but he's also nobody's fool. And neither is Mel. She's intense. Uptight. Sexy. And very, very tempting. Suddenly, Bo's thinking less about revenge and more about kissing and touching and falling into a fly-by-the-seat-of-your-pants kind of forever love. . . .

Chapter 1

If you asked Melanie Anderson, nothing was sexier than flying. Not an eighty-five mile-per-hour ride in a Ferrari, not any chick flick out there, nothing, not even men. Not that she had anything against the penis-carrying gender, but flying was where it was at for Mel, and had been since the tender age of four, when she'd constructed wings out of cardboard and jumped out of a tree on a dare. Unfortunately, that first time the ground got in her way, breaking her fall.

And her ankle.

Her second try had come at age eight, when she'd leapt off her granny's second-story deck into a pile of fallen leaves. No broken ankle this time, but she did receive a nice contusion to the back of the head.

By age twelve, a time when most girls discovered boys and their toys, Mel had discovered airplanes, and had taken a job sweeping for tips at a local airport just to be near them. Maybe because her own home never seemed happy, maybe because she didn't have much else to look forward to, but the magic of flying was all she ever dreamed about.

She wanted to be a pilot. And not just any pilot, but a kick-ass pilot who could fly anywhere, anytime, and look cool while doing it.

Now she was twenty-six and she'd pulled it all off. She ran her own charter service: Anderson Air. That Anderson Air consisted of a single Cessna 172 and a not-exactly-air-worthy Hawker was another matter altogether. Having fueled her dreams from cardboard wings to titanium steel made her proud as hell of herself. Now, if only she could pay her bills, things would be just about perfect, but money, like man-made orgasms, remained in short supply.

"Mel! Mel, sweetie, the oven is kaput again!"

Mel sighed as she walked through the lobby of North Beach Airport, a small, privately owned, fixed-base operation. The cozy, sparsely decorated place was dotted with worn leather couches and low, beat-up coffee tables and potted palm trees— low maintenance to the extreme. A couple of the walls were glass, looking out onto the tarmac and the two large hangars, one of which housed the maintenance department and the other the overnight tie-down department. Beyond that lay a string of fourteen smaller hangars, all rentals. And beyond that, Santa Barbara and the Pacific Ocean, where Mel could routinely find her line guys and aircraft mechanic riding the waves on their surfboards instead of doing their job.

The far wall held a huge map of the world, dotted with different colored pushpins designating the places where she and everyone else had flown to on various chartered flights. Red pins dominated. Mel was red, of course, and just looking at the map made her smile with pride.

Just past the map, the wall jutted out, opening up into the Sunshine Café, an ambitious name for five round tables and a small bar/nook, behind which was a stove, oven, microwave, and refrigerator, all crammed into six hundred square feet and painted a bright sunshine yellow. On the walls hung photos, all of planes, and all gorgeously shot from the ground's viewpoint.

Charlene Stone stood in the middle of the kitchen nook, bottle-dyed maroon hair piled on top of her head, her black lip gloss a perfect match to her black fingernails. She'd turned forty this year and wore a T-shirt that read TWENTY WAS GOOD BUT FORTY IS BETTER, and a pair of short shorts that rivaled Daisy Duke's. As the eighties had been Char's favorite decade to date, she had Poison blaring from a boom box on the counter while staring into the oven. "I can't get my muffins going," she said in her Alabama drawl.

"I thought *I* was your muffin, baby."

This from Charlene's husband, Al, the photographer who'd taken the pictures on the walls, who despite being forty himself had never outgrown his horny twenties. Medium height, built like the boxer he'd once been, he waggled a brow and grinned.

They'd been married forever, had in fact raised two kids while they'd still been kids themselves, but they had empty-nest syndrome now, and were currently revisiting their honeymoon days—meaning they talked about sex often, had sex often, and talked about it some more.

"People come here for my muffins," Charlene said, and smacked Al's chest.

"I love your muffins."

"You're just kissing up now."

This brought out a big, hopeful grin. "No, but I'd like to." He shifted close, put his hands on Char's hips. "Kiss up, and then down . . ."

Char shot Mel a long look. "Men are dogs."

Mel tended to agree with that assessment but she knew enough to keep her tongue. "I'll get the oven fixed."

"Oh, honey, that'd be great. I know you're swamped and this is the last thing you need."

Yep, on the list of things Mel didn't need, the oven going on the blink fell right behind a hole in her head. "We need the oven. I'll get it fixed ASAP."

"Good, because if I keep disappointing the customers, we aren't going to be able to pay our rent this month. Sally will freak."

Ah, yes, the elusive Sally.

Sally was the owner of North Beach Airport, and everyone's boss, from fueling to maintenance to hangaring. Mel herself rented space from Sally for Anderson Air and in return for a lower fee managed the whole airport for Sally. Since Sunshine Café happened to be one of the few profitable segments of North Beach, the broken oven fell into Mel's already-overflowing pot of responsibilities. She pulled the radio off the clip on her belt to call their fix-it guy, who sometimes fixed things, and sometimes didn't. Mostly didn't. "I'll get Ernest."

Charlene sighed.

"Yeah, yeah." Mel brought the radio up to her mouth. "Ernest, come to the café, please."

No answer, which was not a big surprise. No one was sure exactly how old Ernest was but he'd been at North Beach as long as Mel could remember. According to other sources, he'd been around since the dawn of time. Only thing was, he was grumpy as an old goat and was rarely anywhere he should be when Mel needed him.

Like now.

"He's probably rescuing a spider." To Al's credit, he said this with a straight face.

Ernest loved spiders. He actually carried around a special species book in his back pocket so that he could characterize each and every spider he came across, and here just off the Santa Barbara coast, in the shadows of the Santa Ynez Mountains, he came across a lot. The only thing he loved more than spiders was computers. The man, strange as it seemed, was a computer god. He probably could have gotten a job anywhere for more money, but undoubtedly he couldn't nap on the job anywhere else so he stayed at North Beach.

"Ernest," Mel said again into the radio. "Come in, please. Ernest, come in."

"No need to shout, missy."

Mel nearly jumped out of her skin at the low, craggily, grumpy voice behind her. Ernest stood there, all five feet of him packed with attitude, from his steel-toed boots to his greasy trousers and long-sleeved, button-down plaid, to his bad comb-over, which was rumpled now, telling her he'd been sleeping in the storage closet again. The crease on his cheek that resembled the side of a can of oil was a dead giveaway. "The oven's down," she told him.

"Eh?" He cupped a hand to his bad ear. "Speak up!"

Mel would have fired his curmudgeonly ass a long time ago except she couldn't afford anyone else. "Oven! Broken!"

"You never talk loud enough," he grumbled. "Sally's the only one who talks loud enough."

Ernest hadn't actually spoken directly to Sally in years, but arguing with the man was like betting against the house.

Never going to win.

"Can you fix the oven?" she yelled in his good ear.

"I'll fix the damn oven soon as I fix the damn fuel pump!"

Mel's stomach dropped. "What's wrong with the gas pump?" Muffins they could live without. Getting fuel into their customers' aircrafts, some of which landed here daily for the fuel alone, they could not.

"Nothing I can't handle." Ernest was already walking away, his pants slipping down because he had no hips to hold them on. He stopped, hitched them up, then kept moving.

The radio squawked with the announcement of an unscheduled plane arriving in twenty minutes. Mel waited for one of the linemen, Ritchie or Kellan, to respond to the news, but neither did. Once again she lifted the radio to her lips and called for her employees.

No response.

"Gotta love those brain-dead college students," Char said.

Mel resisted the urge to smack her own forehead with the radio. "If those two are in the back hangar getting high again, I'm going to kill them."

"We're falling apart at the seams." Charlene hugged Mel. "Look, honey, you've got your hands full. I'll go see what I can wrangle up without the oven, 'kay?"

"I'll get on it," Mel promised her just as the Poison CD ended.

For one blessed moment silence reigned before a new CD clicked on. Journey. "I just wish we could give this place the makeover it needs," Char yelled over the music.

Mel wished that, too. They were making ends meet, and they all had jobs, two really good things, but no one was getting rich, that was for sure.

Not that she wanted to be rich, but comfortable would be nice . . .

Al followed his wife into the kitchen, his hand sliding down her back to squeeze her ass.

"Albert Edward Stone!" Charlene said in her most Southern-genteel voice. "If you think that instead of cooking muffins, I'm going to 'cook' with you—"

"Come on, just a quickie—"

"That's what you got just last night!"

"Hey, that wasn't a quickie, that was some of my best work!"

Mel covered her ears and walked away. She didn't need the reminder that everyone was getting quickies and she was not. So it'd been a long time for her, so what? People could live without sex.

Or so the rumor went.

"Mel? Mel, are you around here somewhere?"

At Dimi's voice drifting through the lobby from the front receptionist desk, Mel changed direction and headed that way, wondering, what now?

Dimi Wilmington sat perched on the edge of her desk, head tilted as she studied the view out the window of sweeping coastlines bisected by the magnificent Santa Ynez Mountains and a typical low-lying morning fog. Willowy, with legs long past the legal limit, Dimi had a body and face that could launch a thousand ships, make the fat lady sing, and put grown men on their knees to worship at her altar.

She used them to her full advantage, too, rarely coming across a man she didn't like—which probably explained the new whisker burn along her jaw.

Terrific. Everyone was getting lucky except Mel.

It was said she and Dimi were night and day, a modern-day odd couple. Mel being the anal one. The one who gathered worries and stress like moss on a tree. She also tended to gather the heartaches and responsibilities of others much like a fraught mother hen, bitching after all her little chicks, pecking at them until they did as she wanted them to.

Dimi was more a live-and-let-live type of soul. She cared, deeply, she'd just rather light incense and meditate than actually solve a problem. She was both a thorn in Mel's side and her closest confidante.

She wore a multicolored, filmy, gauzy miniskirt and a snug, white cap-sleeved tee with a pink heart in the center that brought the eyes to immediate attention of her brand, spanking-new breasts. But the thing that never failed to amaze Mel about Dimi was that she could go all day and that bright, clean white tee would stay bright, clean white.

Mel didn't even bother to look down at her coveralls, already filthy from just a quick maintenance check on the Cessna. "What's the problem?"

Over the steam of her herbal tea and the faint smoke from the incense she'd lit, Dimi shot Mel a wry smile.

Right. What *wasn't* a problem was a more likely question.

The two of them went back a long ways. As teens, Mel had swept and assisted in the maintenance department, and Dimi had answered phones. Each had been far more at home here than either of their decidedly not *Leave It to Beaver* homes.

Sally Wells, a woman with more dream than cash, had taken them under her wing—Sally, who'd lived as she wanted, wild and free with men and fun aplenty. As their first real role model, Mel and Dimi had both worshipped the ground Sally walked on; Mel appreciating Sally's directness, the way she ran her own show and the world be damned, but for Dimi the worship had gone deeper. She'd wanted to *be* Sally.

Unfortunately, Sally had been unavailable to them for a long time now, and without her around, there was no one for Mel to share the stress of holding all this up with. No one except Dimi. "Tell me," she said to Dimi now. "Believe me, the day can't get worse."

Dimi put her hand over Mel's. "You look tired. You're not drinking that tea I gave you."

"I hate tea. And it's just stress."

"You only hate tea because I tell you it has healing abilities and you think that's a crock of shit." She sighed. "Money's tight again."

"You mean *still*. Money's tight still."

"That's all right." Dimi stood and, primping a little, played with the hem of her skirt, adjusted her top. "We have a couple of hot ones coming in today."

"Hot ones" being Dimi-code for cute, *rich* customers.

"What we have is an unscheduled," Mel said. "I've gotta get out there and do tie-down because God knows where Ritchie or Kellan is."

Dimi pulled out a compact and checked her gloss, ran her tongue over her teeth. "I'll do it."

"Uh-huh." Mel eyed the short, short skirt, which at every move flirted with revealing Dimi's crotch. "You're going to go get your hands dirty, risk that manicure, and tie down a plane? In *that*?"

Dimi smiled. "Should get me a big tip, don't you think?"

"That's not even funny."

"Hey, I'm going to hit on them anyway, might as well get something for it."

"Stop it." Mel knew Dimi was only kidding. Or half-kidding anyway. Dimi enjoyed men the way some women enjoy breathing. "I have enough to worry about."

Dimi sighed and stroked a long, wayward strand of hair from Mel's face. "We'll be fine, hon. You'll come up with something, you always do."

Right. She'd just wave her magic wand and figure it all out. And while she was at it, she'd conjure up a happily ever after for all of them as well. "The oven's down, the gas pump is acting up, and morale's getting low."

"They need a phone call from Sally."

Their gazes met for a long beat.

"You do it this time," Dimi whispered.

"Actually, I was hoping you could, from—" Mel broke off when Ernest appeared out of nowhere, shuffling past the desk, pulling his noisy cart stacked haphazardly with tools and the ever-present jar for liberating spiders.

Mel didn't know how many times she'd asked him not to walk through the lobby like that, to instead go around the outside of the hangar, where customers wouldn't have to see him, but he never listened. At least not to the stuff she wanted him to. "Ernest?"

He'd stopped to stand in front of the vending machine next

to the wall map, scratching his head as he contemplated rows of candy bars. "Yeah?"

"Did you by any chance ever clean out that maintenance hangar, the one Danny wants to stock new parts in?"

"Not yet. Busy, you know."

Right. He looked really busy. She and Dimi waited until he'd made his selection, shoved the candy bar into his pocket next to his spider book, and left.

"I hate the secrets," Dimi whispered.

Yeah, and Mel just loved them. *Not.* She looked at the time. "I gotta go meet that flight. Then I have a flight myself, to LA."

"You're changing your clothes first, right?"

"Yes," Mel said with irritation. "Of course."

"You say that like you don't regularly forget to change from mechanic to pilot. Daily."

Mel rolled her eyes. "I'll be back by two."

Dimi nodded, looked wistfully out the window. "You're so lucky."

"Lucky?" Mel laughed in disbelief. "How exactly?"

"You get to get out of here."

"But you hate to fly," Mel reminded her. "You throw up every time."

"I know, I didn't mean . . ." Dimi searched for words. "Look, don't you ever . . . just want to get in the plane and, I don't know, fly off into the sunset?"

Mel just stared at her incredulously. "Never to return?"

"Well . . . yeah."

North Beach was Mel's home, her *life,* and no, she'd never ever thought about going away and never coming back, and she'd always figured Dimi felt just the same. "Okay, what's wrong?"

Dimi lifted a stack of mail. "Just the usual. Here's your incoming pile. Bills and more bills, if you're wondering, though what's the point of opening them, we still can't pay last month's."

"Officially no one can even bug us until . . ." She glanced at the desk calendar. July ninth. "Tomorrow, the tenth." Oh, God.

"Also we need fuel for the pump, and they won't deliver it without their bill being paid." Dimi leaned over and lit the three candles lining the front of her reception desk. The crystals on her wrists jangled, as did the ones dangling from her ears. The scent of vanilla began to fill the air, joining the incense she'd already lit on the credenza behind her.

"You're going to make people hungry," Mel said. "And the oven's down."

"I'm going to make people feel warm and cozy and at home," Dimi corrected, and smoothed her skirt. "Helps our karma."

Mel wanted to say that she didn't believe in karma or fate, that they each made their own, but the sound of a plane coming in ended the conversation. "They're early." She understood early, she herself was always compulsively early, but it meant she had to run through the lobby, grabbing an extra orange vest off a hook as she went, slipping into the lineman's gear as she moved quickly across the tarmac to greet the plane.

The Gulfstream was a beauty, and her pilot's heart gave one vivacious kick of envy as the plane swept in for a honey of a landing, perfectly controlled by a pilot who was clearly a master of his craft.

When the engine shut off, Mel moved in, squinting against the early chill and wind, using the tie-down blocks to hold the plane steady, her mind wandering as she worked. The oven had gone out twice this month. She needed to look into the cost of a new one. The linemen clearly needed another ass chewing regarding responsibilities, specifically theirs. And then there was the little matter of fuel. She'd have to find a way to pay that bill pronto.

God, her brain hurt.

Finished with the tie-down, she straightened, patted the sleek side of the airplane just for the pleasure of touching it, and blew a stray strand of hair out of her face, wishing she had put on an extra layer of insulation beneath her coveralls because despite it being summer, the early-morning wind off the Pacific cut right through her.

From the other side of the aircraft, the door opened. A set of stairs released. A moment later, two long legs emerged, clad in dark blue trousers, clean work boots, and topped by a most excellent ass. Not averse to enjoying a good view, Mel stayed in place, watching as the rest of the man was revealed. White button-down shirt, sleeves shoved up above his elbows, tawny hair past his collar, blowing in the wind.

Yep, there were a few perks to this job, one of them catering right to Mel's soft spot.

Pilots. This one looked more like a movie star pretending to be a pilot, but you wouldn't hear her complaining. And just like that, from the inside out, she began to warm up nicely.

The man held a clipboard, which he was looking at as he turned, ducking beneath the nose of the plane to come toe-to-toe with her, a lock of tawny hair falling carelessly over his forehead, his eyes shaded behind aviator sunglasses.

And right then and there, every single lust-filled thought drained out of Mel's head to make room for one hollow, horror-filled one.

No.

It couldn't be. After all this time, he wouldn't *dare* show his face.

His only concession to the surprise was a raised brow as he lifted his sunglasses, his sea green gaze taking its sweet time, touching over her own battered work boots, the dirty coveralls, the fiery, uncontrollable red hair she'd piled on top of her head without thought to her appearance. "Look at you," he murmured. "All grown up. G'day, Mel."